# The Samaritan's Friend

# The Samaritan's Friend

JAMES CAMPBELL HUNTER

RESOURCE *Publications* · Eugene, Oregon

THE SAMARITAN'S FRIEND

Resource Publications
An Imprint of Wipf and Stock Publishers
199 W. 8th Ave., Suite 3
Eugene, OR 97401

www.wipfandstock.com

PAPERBACK ISBN: 978-1-6667-5300-4
HARDCOVER ISBN: 978-1-6667-5301-1
EBOOK ISBN: 978-1-6667-5302-8

10/04/22

———————

To Kathryn, who once proofread an important theological paper I
was about to hand in, and
asked me if I wanted to say anything about Jesus.
Turns out, I did.

———————

# Contents

# Acknowledgments

I want to thank all the teachers, pastors, and mentors, who are now part of the cloud of witnesses, that helped me see a gracious, joyously welcoming Jesus.

Thank you, Andrea Lingle. You can paint a scene with your words that sticks with me for a month. As an editor, you couldn't get me on your level, but you helped me do a little better.

Thank you, fellow pilgrims who traveled with me on The Camino and shared table on Iona. You made me think God is really hoping I'll just be myself.

Thank you, hiking gang. Each of you are a gift. It's true that all who wander are not lost, but sometimes we were for sure. And, we survived to make poor decisions another day.

Thank you, Erin and Cammie. You came into my life, awakened my heart, and helped me see that the idea of God throwing someone away is ludicrous.

Thank you, Sarah, Maya, JT, and Michael. You make me want to be the story teller my Grand Daddy Hunter was.

And, thank you Kathryn. God only knows.

# PART 1

# The Wedding

I GUESS THERE'S NO way to see the day coming when your life will completely change, but my life was never even close to the same after I met the traveling teacher from Nazareth.

I met Jesus at a wedding. He was there because his young cousin was the groom. I was there because it meant seven days of free food and wine.

I was something of a wanderer in those days, and a week of free food and wine is a good deal no matter how you look at it. Oh, it wasn't like I was a complete mooch. I had met the young fellow on a construction site, we hit it off, and he had graciously invited me. He just didn't realize how much I was going to eat and drink. Turns out I got a whole lot more out of attending that wedding than a few days without worrying about what I was going to have for supper.

From the very beginning I realized that, when Jesus is present, things change. And no, I'm not just talking about the water-turning-into-wine-thing. I'll get to that in a minute. What got my attention in the very beginning is that I somehow felt Jesus's presence before I saw him. I know that sounds odd and it's hard to explain, but it's like something was added to the air that changed how I saw things. I felt it in my chest. Colors were a little sharper, sounds were a little clearer. I felt a little more joyful, peaceful, courageous even. I realized that I had started smiling, and I couldn't remember why. I just felt good. It's very hard to describe. I just felt him before I saw him. That's all I can tell you.

When I did see him, I knew he was the reason for the feeling. He was a joy to watch. He was an attractive man, in fact, while I would have shied away from the word back then, now I would say he was beautiful. He had dark curly hair, a shorter beard, and deep brown eyes. He was slightly above average in height but not imposing physically. His attractiveness was more about how he carried himself than the way he looked. He was simply enjoying every person, every moment. When you heard him laugh it drew you in and you laughed along without any idea what you were laughing about.

The love between he and his mother was obvious. As I stood watching that day, I saw her light up when she saw him, they both laughed, hers was as contagious as his, then they hugged and shared what sounded like an inside joke, "You're late," she said.

"Nope, right on time."

They hugged one another again, then held each other at arm's length as they gazed into the other's eyes. Then they burst out laughing and hugged one another again.

They laughed. I laughed. The guy next to me looked at me like, "What are you laughing at?" I just shrugged and said, "No idea. Something about being on time."

I watched him as he made his way to the young groom, hugged him and said words that many of the guests had said before, "Prayers for a wonderful life together," but this time it seemed to have a more meaningful, deeper feel to it.

I'm not saying I felt his presence every time he walked up. Several times later on, I was surprised to discover that he had been sitting beside me or walking with me for quite some time without me being aware. But, I am saying that that day, that first meeting, things changed when he got there. I felt it.

I must have been staring noticeably because James, who, like me, had been there with his brother John since the start and seemed to be enjoying the food and wine as much as I was, came up, nudged me in the side, and said, "Want to meet him?"

"Sure," I said. But, to be honest, I wasn't so sure. Along with the scenes of joy and love, something about Jesus made me a little nervous. For some reason I really wanted to make a good first impression. I know it sounds silly but I really wanted him to like me. I wanted him to think I was a good person. I was wishing the wine clouds in my head weren't so thick.

James and I crossed the courtyard, and, when Jesus saw us, he grinned and opened his arms wide to greet James with a hug. That brought a rare smile to the big, deeply tanned fisherman who scowled way more than he smiled. After their embrace, James introduced us, and, even though Jesus was surrounded by family and close friends, I instantly had all his attention. No looking over your shoulder to see who else was around with Jesus. He looked me straight in the eyes, nodding occasionally, smiling at the right times, giving me the impression that he thought what I was saying was possibly the most important thing he was going to hear that day. Like I said, he made me a little nervous.

"It's good to meet you. You're a friend of Isaac's?"

"Yep. Only for a short time. We met on the construction site, where the new market booths are."

"You're a carpenter?"

I smiled, shrugged my shoulders and said, "I can be when I need to eat. I grew up on a farm and you figure out how to do a lot of things on a farm."

"I imagine so. I've done a little carpentry to eat myself. My father taught me—trained Isaac too. A farmer? I have always been interested in farm life, growing things, caring for animals. Maybe we can talk later."

And we did talk later. He made a point of it. He asked me about wheat and olive trees and grapes. He asked about sheep and oxen and plowing.

He noticed the scar on my left arm that I got when I was a little boy because I was standing too close to my father as he swung a sickle. I told him that I was always following my father around and had walked up when he wasn't looking. "Same thing here," he laughed as he pulled up his robe to show me an ugly scar on his shin. "Ax."

He even noticed the bracelet that I wore on that same arm, all I had left that had been my father's. I talked more in that hour or so than I had in two years, but he seemed to be genuinely interested.

We moved from growing things and bracelets to my life's story, and, before I knew it, I had told him pretty much everything. Yep, I had known him for three hours, and I was out of secrets.

I told him all about my father. About how he was such a loving man and was completely open with it. He, like Jesus, apparently, was free with hugs, gentle with animals, talked to fruit trees, and had doted on my mother until her death a few years ago. I told him about my older brother, and how he was a moral and righteous man but not quite so open with his love. I don't know why, but I even told him about the worst thing I had ever done—the time in my life that brought me the most shame. I don't know why or what made me tell him, but I did. It still hurt to think about, let alone talk about, but something just told me that I would be safe telling Jesus. I thought maybe it would help me find some peace to tell the tale. Besides, not talking about it and trying not to think about it hadn't helped. Still, it's hard to tell someone that you're hoping will like you, you broke your father's heart, destroyed your relationship with your brother, and broke pretty much every rule you had learned when you were growing up in the synagogue.

"I was seventeen. Thought the secret to happiness was to do what you want when you want. So, I went to my father and told him that since he had said that the farm would eventually be half mine anyway, I wanted whatever was coming to me right then. I told him that he and my brother would probably make it worth more later, but I'd take my half now and they could have the rest. I don't know what I thought his reaction would be, but

I didn't expect to see the hurt on his face. I hadn't thought about how much it'd hurt him. I was sorry but truly thought I was making sense. 'Look out for number one,' 'Do what makes you happy,' that was my life's philosophy in those days. I thought everybody with any sense thought the same way. Pretty much the only time I was happy was when I was partying, so why not party all the time? It broke his heart but the next week he gave me more money than I had ever seen and I was gone.

"Didn't wait till morning. Didn't even pack. I could buy whatever I wanted when I needed it. I was off that afternoon. Didn't even tell my brother goodbye."

I had been looking at the ground while I talked, so, when I looked up at Jesus, I wasn't going to hold it against him if his expression was one of contempt, but I was surprised to see something more like the look my father had when I told him I wanted to leave. "Where'd you go?" he asked quietly.

I shrugged and said, "Always wanted to see Corinth."

"Corinth?!?" He almost laughed. "Where did that come from?"

"Well, I was seventeen, loved to party, had always heard Corinth was the place to party. Besides, I had all the money in the world. Kinda obvious now that I wasn't too good at thinking things through. Took me about three months to run through every cent I had. Drinking and gambling aren't good investments."

"You were only seventeen, so far from home, what did you do when the money was gone?" There was sincere concern in his question.

I hesitated, because, like I said, I really wanted him to think highly of me, but I was tired of hiding and tired of being ashamed. "A retired Roman soldier got me a job at Aphrodite's Temple. I had lost a lot of money to him and I guess he felt a little bad for me. I was kind of like a maintenance, clean up guy. My pay was shelter at night and whatever food was left over from religious banquets." I couldn't imagine that there was a priest anywhere in Jerusalem who would be willing to pronounce someone clean after he had worked for Aphrodite and ate her food, so, again, I wasn't sure how Jesus would react. He just winced like he, not me, was the one that had been shamed and said,

"I'm sorry."

"Didn't last long," I said. "Cleaning latrines and picking up after their festivals got old fast. One day I just decided enough was enough. I could shovel manure and eat leftovers on my father's farm. Maybe he would let me come back as a servant if I could think of a good enough apology. At least the servants at my father's had regular meals and didn't have to hope the drunk, idol worshipers would leave some of their meal behind. I wanted to go home. Bad."

"So, you went home. It took some courage to do that. Go back and admit you were wrong."

"Didn't feel courageous. Felt embarrassed. Ashamed. Practiced my apology speech for days on the way back."

"How'd it go?"

"Didn't get a chance to use it. I was so anxious to get there that, even though the sun was setting, when I got within twenty or so miles, I walked the entire last night. When I walked through the gate that morning, there was a light fog, and I could barely see the house, but I could see my father. He was up and standing at the door, looking down the road, almost like he was looking for someone, like he was looking for me. When he saw me, he cried out and ran as fast as he could straight for me."

"He ran? Like a little boy?" Jesus was laughing, trying to picture it.

"Yep. Ran so fast he lost one of his sandals, but that didn't slow him down a bit." Jesus laughed again, with obvious delight. I laughed too. Like I said, it was contagious. I laughed even though it was far and away the most tender moment of my life.

"When he got to me, I started my speech, but I didn't get three words out. He put his hand over my mouth and buried his face on my shoulder. He was weeping and laughing all together. Tried to talk, tried to say, 'You're alive' but his throat was too knotted. He finally gave up and before I knew it, he had me inside, gave me fresh clothes, slipped this bracelet on my wrist, and set a meal in front of me that you wouldn't believe."

"What a wonderful story. He loves you very much."

"Well, loved. I'm afraid he was killed by robbers while traveling on a business trip a couple of years ago."

"Oh no!" I thought he might cry, but he gathered himself and said, "What happened with your brother?"

I grimaced, then forced a smile and said, "Well, my brother wasn't as happy to see me as my father was. In fact, he made no secret that he wished I hadn't come home. He never said it out loud, but I got the feeling that, if he had his way, I would have been killed back in the gambling, drinking days.

"About three months after I came home, a man from Samaria brought my father's body to the house and told us what had happened. One week after that, my brother came to me and said, 'Here's three hundred denarii. Take it, leave, and never let me see you again.' That hurt but it was actually pretty generous. It was his farm now, and I could understand how he felt. He had never caused my father a day's grief, other than not forgiving me, and the truth is he had a lot to forgive. I had burned through half our money while he was working hard. I wished I could somehow make it right with him, but it seemed like the best thing I could do was to just take the money and leave. I picked out some sturdy clothes, good walking sandals, threw a couple days worth of food in a bag, and hit the road. That was about two years ago."

I suspected he wondered about my lifestyle since leaving home this time. "I have been a little smarter this time out. Enjoying a quieter life." He looked at the wine cup in my hand. I smiled sheepishly and said, "No, really."

Interestingly, that's the exact moment his mother came and exclaimed, "They're out of wine!"

She was distressed. This was her family, people she loved, and we weren't half way through the festivities. If they were out of wine, they would have to ask everyone to leave. That would be an embarrassment for the young couple and their families that they would never live down.

I wasn't sure what she wanted Jesus to do about it, but she pulled him to the side and an animated conversation ensued. She certainly acted like he needed to do something. Cana was a very small town, and, if the wedding party was out of wine, there probably wasn't enough wine in the whole village to restock it properly. Besides that, Jesus didn't strike me as the kind of person that would be able to buy that much wine even if it was available. I thought about pitching in a little. I had certainly drunk more than my share.

They looked at one another for a moment in silence. I hadn't realized how much they looked alike, especially as one serious face stared into the other. Then Jesus half smiled and said, "I don't think it's time." His mother didn't come close to smiling.

"I'm not playing. This is the only decent meal some of these people will have for weeks." She then turned away and got the attention of three nearby wedding attendants and said, "He's going to need your help. Do whatever he tells you."

Now comes the part that I have no desire to explain or defend. Couldn't if I wanted to. I will only tell you what I saw. You can do whatever you want with it.

Since there had been no room for negotiation or questions in the woman's voice, the confused attendants just stood there. Like statues with puzzled looks on their faces, they looked at Jesus, waiting for instructions. Jesus looked around for a minute and then said, "Fill those stone purification jars with water."

Off to the side of the village's courtyard, next to the small synagogue, there were six huge jars, each capable of holding a bunch of water, maybe thirty gallons. Because there had been so much religious cleansing and washing to prepare for the wedding, they were almost empty, and it was going to be a chore to carry that much water from the village well even though it was in the center of the courtyard, only a few yards away. It took the fellows some time to fill them. In fact, at one point they came to Jesus to say they were done, and he shook his head, smiled, and said, "Fill them till they overflow." So, they did.

I was watching all this plus keeping an eye on the wine supply because it sure seemed to me that filling jars with water wasn't going to help the situation. The last bit of wine at the wedding went into one of the guest's chalice just as the water began to run down the side of the last jar. The steward tugged on his beard anxiously as it dawned on him that there was no more wine to serve.

Jesus walked up to the youngest of the three fellows who had filled the jars, put his hand on his shoulder and said, "Thank you. Now put some in a wine skin and take it to the steward so he can taste it before serving it to the guests."

I don't know who was more baffled, me or the young attendant, but he did as he was told. We both could have fainted when the steward tasted it and said, "This wine is excellent! Why were we waiting till now to bring it out?"

As soon as I could gather myself, I picked up my cup and asked him to pour me some. I stepped away and held the cup in my hand, almost afraid to taste it. I took a sip, and he was right. It was the best wine I had ever tasted, and I had tasted a lot of wine. It not only had a good taste, it kind of made me feel like I did when Jesus first arrived at the wedding. I looked around at the people who were celebrating life and love with their family and friends, and I smiled from my very core. Then I laughed when I realized that there was now enough wine to last for days, far beyond the end of the wedding celebration.

I stood there, lost in the moment for a bit, and then I remembered what I had just witnessed. How in the world had this happened? I looked at Jesus, wondering if he was going to offer some explanation, but he only shook his head in a way that told me that I was going to have to live with the mystery. Then he shrugged and said, "This is the only decent meal some of these people will have for weeks."

I am just telling you what I saw. I've thought about it a lot, and, about all I have to offer is, maybe the lesson is as simple as: Where there is love and concern for others there is enough. Do with that what you will.

One would have thought with the huge new supply of wine that Jesus and the small band that traveled with him would have stayed for a while, but, not long after this, Jesus looked at Peter and said, "It's time to go. Tell the others."

While Peter told the others, Jesus hugged his mother goodbye, put his hands on her shoulders, looked at her, shook his head, and laughed. He then wished Isaac and his bride farewell and walked over to where Peter and the rest were waiting for him.

As they walked away, I wondered where they were going. I wanted to ask. I wanted to talk some more. What I really wanted was for them to take me with them. Just as I was realizing this, Jesus stopped and turned around. He looked at me for a long moment, grinned like he was daring me and said, "You want to come?"

Didn't bother to ask where, "Yes. Yes, I do."

# Infirmities

WE WANDERED AROUND A bit, mostly in the north, but eventually we ended up in Capernaum. I had a feeling that we weren't going to stay long, but Peter had suggested we go to his hometown, and he invited us to stay at his house for as long as we were there.

He had a small house, close to the center of town and within easy walking distance to the Sea of Galilee. If the weather was bad, we would squeeze inside, but mostly we slept outside; some of us on the roof, some on the ground around his door. We tried not to be too intrusive because we wanted to be respectful of Peter's wife and mother-in-law who lived with them, but about a dozen of us were living there. That plus daily discussions with the neighbors pretty much set Peter's house on its ear.

The daily discussions started small, but, as word went through town about Jesus's take on things, it really got crowded. It seemed everyone in town wanted to ask Jesus one of those questions they had always wondered about, "Does the scripture really mean this?" "Why did God do that?" "Why did my loved one die?" "Why is there suffering?" Some of the people who came to hear Jesus were very religious—in the synagogue every week. Mostly though, it was people who never thought much about worshiping on the Sabbath. The vast majority was made up of folks who let others worry about keeping the Sabbath; they had to feed their families. Jesus welcomed them all, and they knew it. He seemed to know everyone's name, and he always remembered their questions and comments from the last discussion. Each person, each comment was valued, and each day more people came.

One morning an obviously distraught Peter met us at the door. "I am afraid there's no breakfast this morning, and we won't be able to have visitors. My mother-in-law got seriously sick last night. We need a physician badly."

"I'll try to find one," said John, James's younger and more pleasant brother, as he quickly rose and started walking toward the village square.

Jesus asked if he could come in and see her, and Peter nodded his head yes. When Jesus went in, I followed. I had learned a little about caring for sick things on the farm, so I thought that I might be able to help.

To say that the poor woman was seriously sick was an understatement. She had been losing fluids in every way imaginable for several hours. She had no color and the smell was horrid. Peter's wife stood beside her bed; her face filled with fear. When Jesus spoke to the sick woman, she tried to answer him, but before she could, she lost consciousness.

"She's been doing that off and on all night," said Peter's wife.

"We need to give her something to drink. Something she can keep down," I said. "I know a mixture that might help. Can we give it a try?" Peter's wife nodded. She was willing to try anything.

Jesus walked over to the bed. Again, it was in bad shape. It was soiled, and the large pile of soiled bedding in the corner told me that there wasn't anything clean left in the house to replace it. Jesus didn't seem to care. He knelt down, took her face in his hands, and whispered something in her ear. She came to and began to violently retch, but there was nothing left on her stomach.

I started for the kitchen area so I could mix the concoction that one of my father's servants had taught me. I heard Jesus talking, and I turned around to see what he was saying.

He was holding the heaving woman, rocking back and forth and saying, "No" over and over. It seemed like an odd thing to be saying. It was like he was gently telling her to stop or more like he was telling the sickness to stop. He just kept saying, "No."

I watched for a moment, but I didn't know what to make of someone telling a sickness to stop, so I went to the kitchen and put my drink together. When I returned about fifteen minutes later, I was stunned. Her color had returned, and she was sitting up by herself. She was still very weak, but the improvement over the course of just a few minutes was, there is no other word, miraculous.

Then I noticed that, while Peter's mother-in-law looked stronger, Jesus looked weaker. He seemed a little disoriented and mumbled to no one in particular, "I said no."

Peter's wife said, "Thank you both for your help and concern, but, please, I need to get this room cleaned." I gave the older woman her drink, helped Jesus to his feet, and we went outside.

I told the others that she was going to be alright (I didn't even attempt to tell them what I had seen and heard), but we would still need to make our own arrangements for breakfast and let the people know that we would not be able to meet at least for that day, probably for a couple of days.

"I really wanted to see Matthew today," Jesus said quietly. I had introduced Jesus to my new friend, Matthew, the day before. Matthew and I had been fishing, mostly for fun, along the lake one day and had hit it off.

When I asked him why he was doing so much better than I was, he told me that he had heard about Jesus and how he was teaching daily. He asked if it would be alright if he came to Peter's house one day and if he did, would I introduce him to Jesus. It seemed odd to me that he would ask permission since half the town was simply dropping by, but I said, "Absolutely, I know he'd be glad to meet you."

"The tax collector?" asked Simon who, like me, was newer to the group.

"Yes, the tax collector. I talked to him a good bit last night. His heart is searching, but he's hurting about something. I want to help if I can."

Simon was a Zealot. His people did not have a good history with tax collectors or anyone sympathetic to the Romans. It was likely that he had vandalized Matthew's property in the past or hurled insults at him and his partner as they collected taxes from the fishermen and other local businesses. We could tell he was having trouble envisioning being kind to a tax collector.

"Well, one thing for sure, tax collectors have a lot of money, and money never hurt any movement. Maybe we can enlist his support." It was Judas talking. I was starting to see that it often came down to money and influence for Judas.

"We can talk about Matthew and tax collectors another time. Right now, we have to get some breakfast and tell the people we won't be here today," said James, who had established himself as one of the senior members of our group. His build and strength gave me the impression that he was used to people doing what he said. He, his brother John, and Peter had known Jesus the longest and seemed to be especially close to him.

"Don't be ridiculous." The voice came from the door. "Breakfast will be ready in a few minutes. We need to get you all fed and this place cleaned up before people start arriving." It was Peter's mother-in-law.

So, we met that day. We spent the morning hearing words of forgiveness, comfort, and challenge to love all, even those we considered enemies. In other words, tax collectors and Zealots were called to be friends. Matthew and Jesus did get a chance to talk. They sat off by themselves for over an hour.

Peter's mother-in-law served everyone there a light lunch, but, after that, Jesus ended the discussion and said he was very tired and needed to take the afternoon off.

As soon everyone was gone, Jesus found his bed and instantly fell asleep. He skipped supper, got up once during the night to throw up, and, in the morning, it was Jesus who was seriously sick. Worse, if you can imagine, than Peter's mother-in-law.

Just as we had feared for the older woman's life, we now wondered if Jesus would survive. John, who had discovered the previous day that the physician was out of town, left mid-morning to get Jesus's mother, Mary. They got back to Peter's just before dark the next day, and Jesus was no better. Most of the time he was unconscious, and, when he was awake, he couldn't keep anything on his stomach, not even the special drink I made for him. The village physician returned but was at a loss. Our concern was growing.

The second evening, we all stood around Jesus's bed and prayed, every one of us wondering if we would ever talk to him again. After a while, Mary asked us to leave the room so she and Jesus could be alone. She said that we all needed to get some rest and she would call for us if anything changed.

I left them as asked but lay down near the front door to be as close as I could. I didn't come close to falling asleep. Around midnight I got up and quietly went to the room where Jesus and his mother were. Jesus was either asleep or passed out, and Mary was sitting quietly on a stool, watching by his side. I didn't say anything; I just walked over and sat down, cross legged on the floor beside her.

For a long time we sat just like that. Then, while still looking at Jesus she said, "He was the most amazing boy. His whole life, more than anything, he wanted to learn about God and live for him. He was always able to see the heart of the teachings, even as a child. Always so kind. Always willing to make friends with anyone. Once, when we were visiting Jerusalem, we were afraid that his willingness to talk to anybody had gotten him in trouble. We thought he had been kidnapped or worse. We searched frantically for three days but then found him, sitting on the temple teaching steps like he was one of the priests. Hadn't even had his bar mitzvah, but there he was asking questions and sharing thoughts with respected teachers from all over. We were furious for the scare he gave us, but he seemed to think that we should have known where he would be and what he'd be doing all along. He did apologize though. That was the only time he ever scared us like that."

We sat for a while longer. Then she started again. "You know, when he was born people we didn't even know came to visit us. Rough local shepherds, rich astrologers from some place I'd never heard of. They said that the heavens changed when he was born. What's a mother supposed to think when someone tells her that? When her baby was born, they saw it in the night sky? When we took him to the temple as a baby, men and women just started coming up to him and blessing him. One old man said, 'When I look at this boy, I know I can die in peace.' Then he looked at me and said that while he would bring great joy and peace to many, he would be the source of great pain for me. I guess I know what he was talking about now. I don't think I can bear a life without my beautiful son in it."

Again, we sat in silence. Then, with a completely inappropriate boldness that comes when you are talking to someone in the middle of the night, I brought up something that wasn't any of my business by any stretch. I figured that I would never have this opportunity again. Quietly I said, "Mam, some of the people say that Jesus's birth was miraculous, that God caused your pregnancy."

She didn't say anything for a number of seconds, and I thought I must have surely crossed the line. I mumbled, "I'm sorry. I know it's none of my business." She made me sit in dark silence for at least another minute. Then I think I detected a slight smile; a gentle yet almost mischievous smile that I had seen on Jesus several times.

"Yes. That is what some say. Of course, some say that Joseph and I were overcome with passion, so Jesus came too early in our marriage. Some say that I broke my covenant to Joseph with a boy from Nazareth but Joseph decided to marry me anyway to protect me from shame. And, some say that a Roman soldier attacked me."

Well, even though I had heard all those things, that conversation was certainly more uncomfortable than I thought it would be. What do you say after that? She smiled again. This time with conviction, "I say, you are right, it is none of your business, but I'll tell you this, of course his birth was a miracle of God. God gave him to us. Not just to Joseph and me, but to you—to everyone—to show us a life that walks in God's way. I say that the life he is living reminds us that God is with us. I say he is a gift. Yes, use the word miracle if by miracle you mean proof God is with us and cares for us."

Suddenly a raspy voice from the bed spoke, "Hello Mother, when did you get here?"

She took his hand and squeezed it tightly, "Sleeping a little late aren't you?" Even though he was very weak, I knew what he was going to say before he said it.

"No mam, waking up right on time."

I was never completely sure what that "right on time" meant. I think it had something to do with living in the now and knowing that all things are good in God's time. In this case, he could have just meant that he was waking up in time to observe Sabbath. He took the day off from teaching, but that evening we had the Sabbath meal and the next morning we headed to the synagogue not far from Peter's house.

# The Synagogue

You could see the roof of Capernaum's synagogue from Peter's front door. It was a little over a quarter of a mile, up a slight hill, in the center of town. Because it was so close, I was surprised when Jesus left a good bit earlier than he needed to, but, since I was ready and had nothing else to do, I walked with him.

Nathaniel, the congregation's leader, and his young daughter, Leah, met us on the porch at the front door. Leah was Nathaniel's only child, the joy of his life, and he made no effort to hide it. Fact is, since his wife had died soon after Leah was born, Nathaniel's life totally revolved around the synagogue and his daughter. Of course, everyone loved Leah. She was a real charmer with a spunk that kept her father's head shaking and everyone else chuckling. She had a beautiful laugh that sometimes drifted into a little snort that only made her and everyone around her laugh more. She was a cutie for sure, perhaps a little plump from her father's doting. She beamed when she saw us coming and hugged us tightly as we made our way up the steps.

Nathaniel was as hospitable a soul as I have ever known. His greeting at the front door each week always made my heart sing with the psalmist, "I was glad when they said to me, 'Let us go to the house of the Lord!'" Somehow, he made everyone feel like it just wouldn't have been the same if they hadn't come.

"Jesus, my friend, so good to see you! I hope you're feeling better. I saw you the other day, you weren't looking so good."

"Ha! Wasn't feeling so good the other day! I'm fine. Looking forward to hearing what you'll give us to ponder this morning."

"Actually, I was thinking, since so many come to the synagogue because of you, I was wondering if you'd be willing to read and teach today. From wherever you want."

Jesus smiled, "Of course. But only if you will share a meal with me later and share your thoughts about the reading and what I have to say about it."

16

"And me? Can I come Jesus?" It was the child. I'll admit that I wondered what a little girl could add to a dialogue between men like Nathaniel and Jesus, but Jesus grinned and said,

"Absolutely, young teacher. I look forward to your insight." And he was serious.

We weren't the first to arrive that morning. Sitting off in a corner was my new friend, the tax collector, Matthew. He was sitting close to a back corner, on one of the benches against the wall. His head was bowed and his shoulders so slumped and sad looking that it was hard to see that he was actually rather tall and strong.

"Hello, my brother!" I called, but Matthew only raised his head briefly and nodded. The morning sunlight highlighted a small stream of tears on one side of his face and the expensive looking ring on his finger when he wiped his cheek. He quickly bowed again.

When I saw the tears, I began to gently walk in Matthew's direction, not realizing that Jesus was right behind me. As we approached, I could hear the tax collector's whispered prayer. "O God, help me, help me. I'm sorry, so sorry. I'm so sorry. Please forgive me. Help me! Help me change, I don't know how. I can't. Please help me." Over and over, it was heart wrenching to hear.

Jesus stepped around me to the weeping man's side. "Matthew, what in the world? My friend, my friend, what's the matter? Tell me what's wrong?" he said with a tone that one might use to settle a frightened animal.

"Jesus, you know what's wrong. I'm wrong! I'm lost, and I don't know what to do. Lost! An abomination they say. That's what's wrong. I'm a god damned abomination, and I don't know what to do!" He said, with a flash of anger that immediately melted back into despair. "I used to be close to God when I was a boy. I loved God and knew he loved me. It was so good. I want that back so bad. I want that back, but, if I'm honest, I don't think I really want to change. What's wrong with me? I want to change. I don't want to change. Don't think I could if I wanted to." He was talking rapidly, like the dam had burst just as we had walked up. I knew what it was like to unload on Jesus and tried to say that with my eyes when he glanced at me. "I love Julius. Can't imagine life without him. I can't give him up. Don't want to lose him. I can't keep living like this though. I need God. I need help. Oh, God help me! What am I going to do?" At first I thought he was talking about being a tax collector, but, when he mentioned Julius, his Roman tax collector partner, I realized he wasn't talking about handling Roman money at all.

Jesus sat down next to his friend, draped an arm around his shoulders, and pulled him a little closer. He began to speak quietly in his ear, and, while

I felt like I was intruding, I strained to hear what my new teacher would say to one so distressed.

"Matthew, listen. Listen to me, Matthew. I am here. I am your friend. And, I say there is no such thing as an abomination. Any name a so-called religious person would call you that makes you feel far from God is a lie. A lie." When he said this, Jesus flashed a little anger himself. "You are a beloved child of God. Wonderfully made. Made in God's image, and when our Father looks at you it's the same way Nathaniel looks at Leah. You are loved," Jesus talked slowly in contrast to Matthew's rapid fire lament. "You have to hear me, you are loved. Even more than Nathaniel loves Leah. Do you think she could do or be anything that would make him call her an abomination? To push her away?"

"Thank you Jesus," mumbled the tax collector. "I know you mean well and you mean what you say, but I'm lost and far from God. I am lost. I can't change. God knows I have tried. Don't know how. Don't want to. Desperately want to. I am simply lost. Cast off. Lost. Hopeless." He said some other things but I couldn't understand him.

"Cast off? Never. And change what, Matthew? What do you need to change? You're honest. You have a tender heart, love people. You're seeking God. There's nothing to change. Even right now, right here, you are turning to God, seeking. You're hurting, but this is turning to our Father. There is nothing left to do. This desire to know God is a wonderful thing. It's God calling. Our Father welcomes you. You are accepted, loved. Don't say you're lost. You're never lost. God doesn't lose people."

Matthew lifted his face to meet Jesus's gaze and said, with a hint of anger, "You know what I need to change, Jesus. You know." Jesus's eyes locked on Matthew's, I could tell his grip on Matthew's shoulder tightened, and he said with, if there is such a thing, gentle sternness,

"Matthew, son of Levi, you know scripture, you know Micah's words, all that God wants from us, 'do justice, love mercy, walk humbly.' Which of those don't describe you? You are fair and just, you are compassionate," now he smiled, "you are probably too humble. In a few days my friends and I will be leaving Capernaum. I want you to come with us. Will you leave your business in your partner's hands and come with us for a while?"

"You're asking me to leave Julius? Leave my business?"

"I am not asking you to leave Julius. Peter and the others that are married are coming. Yes, I'm asking everyone to come away from home and business for a few weeks, maybe months. I know it's a lot to ask, but come with me. Let's walk together. Let's walk with God. I want you to help me tell others that they are loved and accepted. That they are cherished. I want people who have doubts about God loving them to meet you. Will you do that? Will you come with us?"

Matthew returned Jesus's gaze. Looked deep into his eyes. He didn't say anything for several seconds, like he was waiting for Jesus to blink, like he was deciding if he could trust the invitation, "Are you serious? You want me to come with you? Are you sure?"

"I don't say things I'm not sure of." Matthew took a deep breath.

"Yes. It'll take me a few days to arrange some things, to say goodbye. Please, don't leave without me."

"We won't leave for a few days. I won't leave without you."

By now, it was time to start the service. As Nathaniel had indicated, a lot of people were there who hadn't been regular attenders until recently, and it was crowded. Along with the newcomers, one man there was indeed a regular attender, Simon the Pharisee. Simon was wearing a very expensive, bright yellow and red, long-sleeved robe, and his large phylacteries stood out for all to see. He walked strong and straight down the center of the worship space to his usual place in the front of the congregation. He was a large man, and he didn't look happy at all this morning. His lower lip matched his protruding belly, and his bushy eyebrows were furrowed. He looked over at the others with a glare that told me that he didn't share Nathaniel's gladness that attendance was picking up. His sour look got even more sour when Nathaniel started the service and announced that Jesus would be the reader that day.

Perhaps to emphasize what he had said to Matthew, Jesus chose to read from the prophet Micah, "He has shown you . . . what is good . . . To act justly and to love mercy and to walk humbly with your God." Then he shared a message with us that I suspected wouldn't have played too well with the teachers in Jerusalem. He talked about God loving everyone, and he warned that if we start thinking only of ourselves as special and others further from God, we would be off track. He said that looking on others with mercy helped us to receive mercy ourselves, and it may be that we need more mercy than the folks we want to look down on. He didn't say much about keeping rules; he talked about a changed heart, a loving heart.

That may not sound very radical and deep, but it wasn't the usual fare in most religious discussions. More often than not, religious folks talked about rule keeping, what you should do and what you couldn't do. That's the kind of stuff Simon the Pharisee liked. I know this because after the service he pretty much told Jesus as much.

"Jesus, I am very disappointed if you are saying that there is no benefit to being a child of Abraham and following the commandments. That's the way I was taught, in Jerusalem, by the best teachers. I think you'll find that our leaders in Jerusalem agree with me. I've studied hard and sacrificed a lot. Unlike you, I don't just tell people what they want to hear. Of course, there is a difference between those that keep the law and those who don't. I am not an adulterer, a thief, a drunk, and certainly not anything like that tax collector, the one who lives an unspeakable life with that heathen Roman. I saw you talking to him before the service, your arm around him. You need to spend more time teaching people about things like fasting, tithing, and keeping the commandments and stop giving them a false sense of security."

"Simon, apparently you were paying close attention to what I was saying. Thank you for listening. I believe some of what you are saying is true," was Jesus's only response.

As we walked back to Peter's house, Jesus called Simon the ex-Zealot to come beside him, "Simon, I have a question for you. Whose heart do you think is closer to God's, Matthew, our tax collector friend, or our Pharisee friend that shares your name?" Simon just nodded and smiled. He was new to the group, but he had been around long enough to know the answer to that one.

# Simon's Table

THE INVITATION TO SIMON's house was a surprise. At least it was for me. Simon was a Pharisee, and Jesus, well, Jesus wasn't. Simon was very careful about doing things the right way, very concerned about who was in right standing with God. For Simon, some people were in and a lot of people definitely were not. Jesus wasn't particularly careful about the correct way to do things, and I am not sure he considered anyone out.

I'm not saying that Jesus wasn't religious. He was very religious, just in a way that I had never seen before. He was the most prayerful person I have ever known, and he taught people to pray in a way that completely changed their lives. Jesus went to the synagogue every Sabbath and knew the Holy Scriptures better than the oldest and most studious of teachers. It's just that he seemed to ignore a sizable amount of it.

For many, especially folks like Simon, he was a little too forgiving and way too inclusive. Some of the religious leaders had begun to openly wonder where the lines were for Jesus. They wondered if there were any lines at all. Simon and his friends liked lines.

On top of this, Jesus's lifestyle was disturbingly simple. Most people see money and possessions as a way to keep score, signs of God's favor. Jesus, even though he was a skilled carpenter, didn't care to keep a steady job. He had one robe. It was a nice one, well made and sturdy, but it was pretty much the only thing he owned.

A couple of days earlier we had moved over to Matthew and Julius's house because of its size. After the servant who had delivered the invitation to Simon's house left, Matthew was the first to speak. He made it clear that there was no way he was going.

"Simon hates me! I've known him all my life. He's bullied me since I was a child and hates me even more now that I collect taxes. There is no way I am spending a minute with him that I don't have to, let alone an entire evening!"

Julius put his hand on Matthew's shoulder and gave a gentle rub-pat combination. Jesus looked at him with a sympathetic expression and said, "Nobody has to go. But, I am. I've been invited."

"Well, I am certainly going," said Judas. "This is just the kind of connection that we have been waiting for. It's a great opportunity. If we could count Simon as a supporter of our movement, it would give us all kinds of credibility with the Pharisees and the leaders in Jerusalem. I know some of you disagree, but we need leaders like this on our side. If we can get influential leaders, if we can get the people behind us, and if we have enough funding, we'll be hard to stop. Then we can really make a difference."

That said, everyone else, except me, decided that, if Matthew didn't have to go, they didn't have to go either. So, it was just Jesus, Judas, and me who went to break bread at Simon's table. I wasn't trying to make connections, and I wasn't being polite. I just figured that listening to Jesus and Simon go at it over how to interpret Moses was a pretty good way to spend an evening. Besides, the idea of another night of Peter's specialty, biscuits and fish, wasn't very appealing.

Even though Simon and Matthew lived in separate worlds, their houses were fairly close. It was a short walk up the hill, through a crowded street to our host's home. As we walked, some of the neighboring children ran up to get a head rub or a quick tickle from Jesus. Even the older ones, who thought they were too mature for head rubs, caught themselves smiling when Jesus teased them and winked at them. This kind of thing always irritated Judas but Jesus loved it. I used to feel like Jesus and Judas were perplexed, to say the least, by one another. It seemed like they wanted to be close but could never quite pull it off.

Simon was standing just outside the door, his arms folded, waiting for us when we arrived. "Good, you're here," he said to Jesus without much warmth. Then he looked at Judas and me and seemed to be wondering what to do about us. It occurred to me that the invitation was only meant for Jesus, but he let us in.

When the servants came from the back of the house to welcome us, Simon waved them off and ushered Jesus to his assigned place. It was the one to the right of the seat of honor. He took the highest seat himself, leaving Judas and me to recline wherever we found an open spot. Judas didn't seem to mind. He was beaming and telling Simon what a nice home he had.

"Simon, your courtyard is beautiful. So green and so many nice trees." Judas gushed. "Is your house the largest in town? The house on the other side of the courtyard, where your servants stay, is larger than the one I grew up in."

Judas went on to tell Simon how much he admired his education and lifestyle, and he had been so looking forward to the evening. I was admiring the delicious looking food on the table. Jesus was quietly taking it all in, smiling slightly. He was the same everywhere he went. It didn't matter if he was at Simon's or sharing a simple meal with the poorest family in town. No, that's not entirely true. The atmosphere was lighter with the poorer folks. There was more laughter. I guess that was because that's the kind of home he grew up in.

It was a wonderful meal. It had everything one would expect: good wine, fish, and bread so tasty it made me wonder what Peter was doing wrong when he baked. There was lamb, fat olives, cucumbers, melons, onions, pomegranates, figs, and frankly a couple of things that I didn't know what they were, some kind of Egyptian pastry according to Simon, but all of it was exquisite. Simon assured us that everything had been washed and prepared properly, according to tradition. I don't think any of us really cared, but we thanked him for letting us know.

We had been eating for a few minutes, Simon had just asked Jesus how he normally observed the Sabbath, when Rachel burst in off the street. While I wasn't sure if Judas and I had been invited, I was positive Rachel had not.

I only knew her by reputation, and I'm afraid her reputation wasn't all that great. She was single and that usually meant hard times for women, but she could somehow afford a nice house, lots of jewelry, and lots of parties. Lots of parties. I had seen her many times dancing and laughing in the street outside her house.

I'll admit I was intimidated by her wealth and loudness but even more by her beauty. She had dark hair with a reddish tint, green eyes, and a round here, thin there body that was completely distracting—intimidating.

"Teacher, they told me you were here. I'm sorry, but I just had to see you tonight. I couldn't wait. I, I just had to see you, to thank you." Her words and voice were uncharacteristically timid, but her stance was one of resolve. She knew she wasn't welcome. It was pretty easy to tell that if you looked at Simon's scowl. His feelings were clear. But, it was just as clear, she wasn't going anywhere. I was surprised when I saw tears welling up in her eyes. Soon she was crying, then she began to weep and sob, then her legs wouldn't hold her any longer, and she fell at Jesus's feet. She gave up trying to put together sentences in a comprehensible way. Between sobs she kept saying, "Thank you, thank you for spending so much time talking to me, for helping me see. I'm sorry to be making a scene. I just got it. I was sitting home praying like you taught me and thinking about what you said, and I just got it, really got it. I am his daughter and loved. Do you know how impossible that seems to me?"

Then she took a bottle of very expensive balm from her bag and rubbed all of it on Jesus's feet. She then began to kiss his feet as if he were a king or something, and when she noticed that her tears were wetting him, she wiped his feet with her hair.

Jesus gently took her face into his hands and tilted her head up until they were looking into each other's eyes. It was what we had started calling "the look." We had seen it many times before. Matthew had gotten a version of it in the synagogue.

Jesus had dark brown eyes, very dark. When he was serious, you hoped he wouldn't look at you. You knew the gaze would be too intense. You were certain that he would see through every mask and know all your secrets— every sin, every shameful act or thought. But then, when he did look at you, it wasn't like that at all. Yes, he saw right through you and he saw all that stuff, but it wasn't with harshness or judgment. It was kindness, hope, and possibility. For the person getting "the look" it was happy surprise, joy, and love, even delight, all mixed together. When Jesus gave you "the look," you were stunned to realize that he thought you were, well, just wonderful. He looked at Rachel this way. It just made her cry even more. Now the tears were falling on his hands.

Judas was aghast. His plans for the evening were exploding. But aghast doesn't even touch what Simon was. He was furious, beyond furious. He stood up and clenched his fists by his sides as he shouted, "I cannot believe you let that woman touch you! I cannot believe you let her in my house!"

Things were getting intense, fast. Even so, I couldn't help but chuckle a little on the inside. I was thinking about Rachel being in Simon's house, at his table, and how that would give his neighbors something to talk about for quite a while. I think he may have been thinking the same thing but failing to find it as humorous as I was.

"I invited you here so I could learn more about your teaching. I guess I know all I need to know now! If you let people like that touch you, if you touch people like that, you are certainly no teacher that I want to listen to! Woman, get away from my table! Get out of my house! Now!"

Jesus put his hand up, "Simon, wait." Everything seemed to de-escalate when he spoke. Simon was beside himself, but Jesus somehow took control of the room. His calm was simply stronger than Simon's fury. But I had a feeling it wouldn't last. "Simon, I would very much like to share something with you. Something I had to learn myself. Frankly, it may help you see things more clearly. See others in a different way."

Simon almost snorted but he said, "Please do."

"Sit back down. Let's talk. Simon, I am not sure why you really invited me here this evening, perhaps to respectfully discuss the law as equals, per-haps to try and catch me in some error. Either way, I'm glad Rachel is here. She's showing us the kingdom. Her presence at your table can be a gift if you will simply see her, not as what you seem to be thinking about her, but as a beloved child of God, just like you and me. A child of God that has a gift for you if you will receive it." Simon sat back down but had a look on his face made me doubt he was open to new insight. Rachel sat down as well. Her head tilted a bit and a smile formed on her face when Jesus called her a beloved child of God.

Jesus continued, "Growing in God's way almost always involves seeing that the Father's love is greater and wider than we thought. You might not believe it, but I used to be very strict. I was very careful about who I associated with and how I did things. I spent many years separated from society, living with the people by the Dead Sea. In fact, until a few months ago, I was convinced that God only wanted me to be a teacher for the people of Israel. Then I met a woman in Tyre." I noticed that his eye had caught something over Simon's shoulder. When I followed his line of vision, I saw that one of Simon's servants, a young man, almost a boy, had quietly moved closer to hear what Jesus would say about Rachel's presence. Jesus looked at me, gave me a little nod and wink concerning the young servant. Then he said, "I bet you remember the woman I'm talking about."

Oh yes, I remembered her. I was the one who told Jesus he needed to do something about her. I told him to send her away. I couldn't figure out why she was bothering us in the first place. She wasn't a Jew, and Jesus was a Jewish teacher. We worship the God who is, and she worships who knows what? All I know for sure is that she had a necklace with a small image of Melqart, the protector god of Tyre, around her neck. She did call Jesus, "Son of David," but I wasn't buying it. I figured someone had told her to use that phrase because it might flatter Jesus into helping her.

She wanted help for her young daughter. I'll admit the poor girl touched my heart. She was in a pit of despair, half in, half out of reality, cutting herself with rocks, and refusing to take any nourishment. But what were we supposed to do? What business did this foreign worshiper of Melqart have with us? Why didn't she leave us alone? Besides that, the woman had no social graces. She had to know that it wasn't proper for us to even talk to her, but she just kept pushing, kept saying that she wasn't leaving until she saw Jesus. Finally. I went to Jesus and said,

"You've got to do something. Send her away, she won't listen to us."

So, Jesus tried. "Woman, we are all Jews and my mission is to the people of Israel. There's nothing I can do for you."

"That's just stupid!" (I told you she had no social graces.)

"It just wouldn't be right to take children's bread and give it to dogs." When he said this we all figured that would be an end to it. I don't see how he could have been clearer, but she wasn't deterred at all. Without missing a beat she said,

"Even the dogs get the crumbs that fall off the table." Well, that changed the entire conversation. We looked at her and saw her for the first time. Jesus was telling Simon all this and then he said something I hadn't heard him say before.

"Simon, when that woman said that, when she was literally willing to call herself a dog to help her daughter, it embarrassed me and made me look at her like I'm asking you to look at Rachel.

"I saw her as God's child. I saw her as one created 'fearfully and wonderfully.'" Rachel audibly gave a small gasp and tears welled up again. She gave Simon a quick look to see how he was receiving her being referred to as God's child. Unfortunately, when she saw his face, he wasn't buying and was still angry. The joy on her own face dimmed. Jesus noticed this, I saw his jaw tighten, but he continued, "The scripture talks about how we are knit by God in our mother's womb. Do you think that those words are only meant for Jews, only for those who believe a certain way? Do you think that only the people of Israel love their children? Are we the only ones that love our children enough to do anything we can to help them when they need us? Don't you think that God, who knows when a sparrow falls, knows when a woman of Tyre weeps? When I saw her like this, of course I prayed for her daughter."

Simon still wasn't buying it. Not even close. "I think that's worse than talking to this woman tonight! There has to be some kind of boundary or else there is no reason for the Law and commandments. There have to be rules! If prostitutes and idol worshipers are welcome, then why follow any of the commands? Jesus, you are trying to destroy all that is good and right about our religion."

"No Simon, you have dedicated your life to God, and I'm sure you are wise in many ways, but I am afraid you don't understand the most important things. The Law was given to us to help us worship and to keep us from hurting one another. We aren't supposed to use it to exclude and hurt others. You should know this as well as I do. Everything comes under the greatest commands: to love God and love our neighbors as part of ourselves. Every religious practice is supposed to help us fulfill these two things."

Simon's anger was rising again, "You are trying to twist scripture. I don't know where you get these ideas, but they aren't true. We have hundreds of years, thousands of years, of tradition to teach us the way. We honor God when we are willing to be different and separate ourselves from sinners like this woman." Simon said "this woman" like he was cursing and now Jesus was agitated.

"Simon, you invited me to your table to talk about scripture, but you are unwilling to live it. You barely gave us a welcome when we got here even though we came on your invitation. Here's what you need to know: God is God for all. You cannot welcome me into your home without also welcoming Rachel. You and I don't get to pick and choose those who are called God's own."

"Have it your way, Jesus. If you are with her, then you both need to leave." Simon's red face, strained voice, everything about him, showed that he had nothing but contempt for Jesus. He stood again for emphasis, certain that he was right and Jesus was wrong. It was impossible for him to believe that what Jesus was saying was true.

Jesus nodded at Judas and me and we rose to leave. Judas's shoulders slumped, he sighed deeply, looked sheepishly at Simon, and slowly stood. Simon just glared.

Jesus took Rachel by the hand to help her up, and we began our walk back to Matthew's.

# The Life of Prayer

JESUS AND I HAD one thing in common. We both liked to get up before sunrise. I did because that is how I was brought up. On the farm the day started long before the sun's first rays peeked over the horizon. Even though farm life was far behind me, when I got up early, I felt close to my father. Most mornings I would sit in the dark, face the direction of my old home, and ponder life; ponder what had happened, what I wish had happened. I would relive better times with my father and brother and wonder if my brother ever thought of me. Jesus got up early to pray.

One morning, when it was just us, I blurted out, "I'm not much of a prayer guy." Jesus was quiet but I knew I had his full attention. "I mean, I pray but mostly because I feel like I ought to. I run out of things to say. My mind wanders, and I get distracted. And, I'm sorry, but I just don't feel anything. I get bored.

"Like I said, not much of a prayer guy."

"Wanna be?"

The question kind of startled me. I meant to be simply stating a fact. I just felt like telling him why I sat staring off into space while he prayed. I figured that was just the way it was. He seemed to be suggesting that I could change. I pondered that for a moment, but then I just decided to tell the truth. I wanted whatever it was that made Jesus look forward to morning.

"The other night, at Simon's, when Rachel came in, she said you taught her to pray. She said that, when she was praying, she felt love. I only feel like it's a chore. I'm supposed to pray, I guess. I need to pray, so I pray, sorta. Can you teach me to pray in a way that gives me that kind of feeling?"

"Nope. I'm sorry. I can't give you some special words that'll make that feeling happen. Things like that are just gifts. We don't have control over them, but sometimes they happen. Sometimes.

"And, just so you know, we don't have control over where our thoughts go either. Minds wander. Mine does—often. All we have control over is whether we will pray or not. Sometimes our minds wander. Sometimes we don't feel anything. But we're invited, and we're loved." He smiled and added, "So keep practicing."

"But you told Rachel something. You didn't just say, 'Keep practicing.' She said you taught her. What'd you teach her?"

He smiled again and said, "If you'll think about it, it's probably stuff you already know." I was starting to feel a little frustrated. I'm sure he didn't miss my sigh.

"Teacher, I promise, if I already knew it, I wouldn't bother you by asking."

"OK, it'd probably be better if you wrestled with this yourself, but here's what I told her." He motioned for me to come sit closer to him, and I moved to a large stone about five feet from where he was sitting. "I told her that prayer is built on remembering what is deeply true and making our best requests. I told her to sit for a minute and think about what she was absolutely certain was true about God. Then think of one or two things she wanted to say. One or two things she wanted to make sure Abba heard if he didn't hear anything else. Start there. Then remind yourself that God loves and cares for all. God is our father, Abba, Friend, and not just yours or mine but everyone's. Everyone's and all things." As he said this, without thinking, he held his arms as if he were about to receive an embrace. He took a long slow breath before continuing, and I realized he wasn't just teaching, he was praying as he taught.

A raven landed a few feet from us and a couple of sparrows hopped closer. I told myself that they weren't actually listening and were only willing to be so close because we had been still so long. Still, I wouldn't have been totally surprised if one of them flew up and perched on his shoulder.

"Then we remind ourselves that we can trust God's love. We lean into that and say we want his will to be done, not ours. That's the first prayer I remember my mother teaching me. 'Your will, not my own.' She lives that prayer. She's always willing to let go of her plans to follow God.

The raven flew off. I guess that was enough for one day. Jesus watched him as he headed to the top of a distant tree and let out three caws. I sat, waiting for him to continue and felt a gentle wind.

"Next, we pray for help to make it through the present day. Sometimes we want to pray for things that are far off in the future that may or may not happen. That's okay, but it's best to focus on the present. Ask for what you need to be faithful today.

"And when you pray be sure to also remember that God will change your heart to be loving and forgiving, just as his is. The best way to do this is to not only remember the things you wish you had done or not done, but also think about the people that you need to forgive. Trying to forgive others changes our hearts. We begin to realize that God's nature is to be tender-hearted and forgiving." I thought about my brother. I thought about some Greeks that had made me the butt of their jokes during some of my lowest days in Corinth. Maybe Jesus couldn't promise praying would be fun but he certainly made it challenging. And, as if on cue he said, "Finally, simply ask for help. Walking in the way is hard. There are many things that could distract us and hurt us. Only God can keep us on the path.

"If you pray like this, seeking God in humility, as you truly are and not pretending to be something you aren't, and God as he truly is and not as you wish him to be, that is praying in Spirit and truth.

"That's pretty much what I taught Rachel." He stood up and took a step toward me. When he got close enough, he gently shoved my shoulder, "Keep practicing." He chuckled and started back for the house.

That was a lot to digest. I sat in silence, trying to remember every word as the sun separated itself from the horizon and a new day began.

Later that day, I saw what those words looked like when they are lived out and not just said. It was our friend, Simon the Pharisee, that helped this happen. I thought for sure we were done with him after the scene with Rachel at his house, but I have since learned that people like Simon never let things go.

It was about midday when he burst in, uninvited, during a meal. Jesus, Matthew, and I were sharing a little fish and bread when there he was at the door with six of his friends. Three of them had swords.

"Jesus, I'd like a word." He said it loudly, not as a request. I did detect a sneer in Matthew's direction, but he ignored me; just as he had the other evening at his house.

Matthew and I scrambled to our feet, but Jesus stood slowly, took a moment to look at each of the men, and said, "Of course Simon, what can I do for you?"

"This is not a social visit."

"I can tell."

"You would do well to listen carefully to what we've come to tell you."

"I will." Jesus was not intimidated. His hands hung loosely by his side and his hands were open, not clenched. His head was slightly cocked like he was very interested in what Simon was saying and didn't want to miss anything. It was like he and Simon had bumped into each other at the market and were discussing the damage to Simon's garden due to last night's storm. Simon didn't seem to appreciate this. I noticed a vein near his temple that I hadn't seen before.

"Jesus! You have no respect for our traditions! You ignore Moses's rules for righteous living and teach others to do the same." Simon's right fist was clenched tightly, and he shook it at Jesus. "We are here to tell you to stop."

"Simon, I honestly believe that I'm not ignoring anything Moses left us. I'm trying to fulfill his teachings—and the words of the prophets."

"That's ridiculous! You break rules to suit yourself and lead the worst sinners and even Gentiles to believe they are accepted in God's sight!"

Jesus didn't answer him for a minute. An awkward minute. I noticed a fly on my last piece of fish and wanted to wave it off with my foot, but I wasn't sure a sudden move would be wise. To distract myself from the fly, I looked at the sky through the door and noticed that a storm was brewing in the heavens as well.

Jesus finally replied, "The truth is, Simon, you are partly right. You are wrong when you say that I break rules on a whim. I'm seeking to make everything I say and do a part of following God's desire for justice and mercy. But, I do want those you call sinners, and, yes, Gentiles, to know that God loves them and that they are God's children, just as you and I are. Elijah ministered to a Gentile widow. Elisha healed a Gentile leper. The prophet Isaiah speaks of foreigners from the east, west, north, and south being in God's favor. He says mercy is for young and old, servant and free, male, female, eunuchs . . . everyone. I am not breaking God's law. In fact, I'm hoping to remind you, and others who think like you, what it is." My eyebrows raised involuntarily.

"No!" Simon was beyond shouting and no one could miss that vein now. "What you are saying is dangerous." He emphasized each word, almost spitting them. "It is dangerous to the very life God has given us. We cannot allow this kind of teaching to go on. It will corrupt our children and ruin our religion. You'll see Jesus, God will prove us right. There will come a time when no one remembers you and all will see that we are the righteous ones."

"Simon, don't be so afraid that you can't hear."

"I am afraid of lies, but it is you who refuses to hear! Read the Psalms, they say, 'I have not sat with the wicked and I despise the company of evildoers.' There have to be standards. There have to be boundaries, or else we have nothing. Things will fall apart." Now both Simon's fists were clenched, his eyes darting from Jesus to the men he was with. His breath had gotten louder and faster. His agitation made him look like he had aged ten years in the last three minutes.

"Simon, please hear me," Jesus's voice was calmer. The contrast between the two was immense. "Evil doers are not the ones who drink too much or don't pray the right way. They are certainly not the poor who wonder each day if they'll have enough to feed their families. Read it again. The evil doers are the powerful who ignore and trample the weak. It says don't sit and fellowship with people like that. Don't be numbered with them. That's what you look like when you burst into someone's home with swords." I wished he hadn't said that last part. I was more than a little nervous about Simon and his friends with swords. Something told me that the three men with swords knew how to use them.

"Jesus, I will tell you one last time. Stop spreading these lies. Stop pretending that you are speaking for God, or we will stop you, and God will be on our side when we do."

"Simon, let me be clear. I am not teaching what I am because I desire anything, certainly not your enmity. I believe, 'The Spirit of the Lord is upon me, because he has anointed me to bring good news to the poor. He has sent me to proclaim release to the captives and recovery of sight to the blind, to let the oppressed go free, to proclaim the year of the Lord's favor,' I would like for you to join me."

When Jesus said this, Simon looked at the men with swords and nodded. They pulled their swords out, and, I was right, it wasn't the first time they had pulled those swords with the intent to use them. In sync, the three with swords took a strong, balanced step toward us.

"Jesus, we are going to take you and your friends if they try to stop us. We're going to take you outside town and give you a false prophet's reward." They were going to kill him! No! I was not even close to a swordsman, but, yes, they were going to kill me too because I was not going to just stand there and let these idiots kill the best man I had ever known. I stepped to meet them, frantically looking around, trying to find something that would pass for a weapon.

Jesus touched my arm and I stopped. He turned to Simon and the others. "No. I don't think you really know what you are doing, but I am not surprised that this is what you want to do. I also won't be surprised if one day you or someone like you does something like this, thinking that they are on God's side. But, not today. Today I am having dinner at Rachel's. She is looking forward to it. I don't want to disappoint her." He looked each of them in the face, opened his hands, extended his arms a little with his palms toward them, made a gentle shooing motion like he was asking hens to leave the house, and said, "You have said what you wanted to say; now you need to leave."

They stared at him in disbelief for a moment. And then, they just turned and left, muttering something about Jesus being a lunatic. I do not know why they left. Maybe it shamed them to see him standing there, harmless. Maybe there was something in his voice that made them lose their appetite for violence. Maybe it was just one of those things Jesus did that I will never understand. All I know is that they left.

Jesus sat back down, took a loaf of bread, gave thanks, broke it, and offered a piece to Matthew, then me. We took it and ate in silence.

I am not sure what Matthew was thinking, but I had the feeling that one of the truest things spoken that day was when Jesus said that there may come a time that he would have to prove his commitment to his message with his life. I thought about what he said about his mother and the will of God, that she puts it above everything, even what she wants.

# Samaria

FOLLOWING JESUS MEANT MOVING around. "Let's go," may have been his favorite two words. When we were traveling, we were outside more than inside, and Jesus loved it. Jesus loved the land, its history and its holy places. Often, he would stop and retell the ancient stories at the spot where they happened. "Joshua crossed the river near here . . . David probably hid in this area . . . Elijah prayed on this mountain."

Just as much, perhaps more, he loved nature. There was no telling what would catch his attention and become an object lesson: a simple flower, a little bird, a wet stone reflecting the sun after a rain. When we walked through fields gleaning our meals, as wanderers do, he would pick the fruit with reverence and gratitude.

A favorite thing was to look at the sky, call one of us by name, and say, "Can you hear it?" He would be smiling like he was teasing, but I'm not so sure he couldn't hear something, some deep song that we were missing. One night I asked why he kept doing this. He grinned and said, "If 'the heavens are telling the glory of God,' it's good to listen now and then."

The sky wasn't the only thing he listened to. He always had time to hear somebody's story. The people he would spend an afternoon or evening with were a constant surprise. He had a knack for finding the loneliest, the most beat down, and often, the most sinful person in the village. Sometimes, this didn't seem like a good gift to have.

For example, once when we were staying in Bethany, he and I left the others at our friend Martha's house and headed to the market to buy some things for our evening meal. As we walked down the road, a Roman soldier who smelled like he had been drinking for a week grabbed Jesus by the shoulder and snarled, "Hey you, I need a good strong Jew to carry my pack."

Jesus stopped and said, "Sure. I'll carry it. Maybe we can talk while we walk." I didn't think trying to make friends with a drunk soldier was the best of ideas and tried to get Jesus's attention without the soldier noticing, while I made a face and shook my head no. Jesus either didn't notice or chose to ignore me. "Maybe you can tell me a little about yourself, where you grew up, and how you became a soldier. I'll bet you have some good stories."

He may have been drinking, but he was a trained warrior. He was so fast Jesus didn't have time to flinch before he had backhanded him across the face. "You stupid ass! My house is three miles from here and you're only required to carry my pack one! Didn't your mother bother to teach you Roman law? We give you peace and protection. You obey and help us when we ask. Because we are benevolent and kind, you only have to carry our packs one mile. Damn! I am tired of the constant stupidity in this place! I don't want a stupid Jew to chat with. I want you to carry my pack!" He looked down at the hand he had used to hit Jesus, chuckled and mouthed the words benevolent and kind to himself, savoring his little joke. "So, right now! Pick it up, shut up, and let's go."

I had never seen Jesus angry but the shock of the insult and the sudden pain sparked a fire that frightened me. I had also never noticed how strong he looked. His fist was clinched and the muscles in his forearm looked like thick cords. It occurred to me that the soldier, trained as he was, may have bitten off a little more than he could chew, at least more than he could chew easily. I'll admit I was afraid. I had seen men dying as they hung from Roman crosses for sedition. Getting into a fist fight with a soldier was probably sedition.

But, quicker than the soldier's fist, Jesus's anger left. He picked up the soldier's pack, threw it over his shoulder, smiled through swelling lips and said, "Three miles isn't that far. I'll see you get home okay. We can talk or not talk; your choice."

The soldier looked at him like he was crazy. I did too. I thought about leaving them and heading back to Martha's but decided it wasn't a good time to leave Jesus alone. Off we went. The whole three miles. When we got to the soldier's home, we knew all about his little Italian hometown, his father who had also been in the Roman army, and how his favorite place he had ever been stationed was Ephesus because he liked the library. Turns out our besotted new friend was quite the student. Jesus got a chance to tell the soldier that along with the basics of Roman law, his mother had also taught him to pray for the strength it takes to forgive. We were invited in for a snack and a little first aid for Jesus's face.

Like I said, he had a knack, a sometimes scary, knack.

I guess to most folks it seemed like we were just wandering around, sometimes east, sometimes north, sometimes to Jerusalem for holy days, sometimes skipping them. Just meandering, waiting to bump into a Roman soldier, or a beggar, or a widow, or a confused religious leader. But, it never felt directionless to me. I always had the impression that we had a destination, like we were headed to an appointment that only Jesus knew about. So, it surprised us one morning, after we had finished breakfast, when Jesus asked us which way we wanted to go. We were camped just south of Samaria, and Jesus asked, "What do you all want to do, go east around Samaria or go straight through?" Even though we weren't used to giving input on where we went, there were some pretty quick answers.

"Go around!" said Simon. "They hate us. To be honest, I don't like them much either. No reason to be around them if we can avoid it."

"We don't need to be hanging around Samaritans. They've nothing to do with us. I don't want to be seen with them," added Judas.

The others were pretty much with Simon and Judas. James and John felt the need to throw in a story about how a Samaritan teenager had stolen some fish off their boat. I sure hoped the young fellow got away. In those days, James had a reputation for having a pretty bad temper, and I had heard some pretty graphic stories about how rough James could get. I was pretty sure all the scars on his hands and a couple on his face weren't from fishing accidents.

"So, we're agreed?" asked Jesus. "That's how we feel about Samaritans? We'll head east?"

I hadn't said anything yet. I never really felt like I was enough "in" the group to have too much of a say about such things, but I couldn't let that pass. I am pretty sure Jesus wasn't surprised when I spoke up. In fact, I think he was expecting me to. "No. I'm fine walking through Samaria. I don't have anything against Samaritans. In fact, a man from the village near Jacob's well once showed my family a great kindness."

"A kind Samaritan? What did he do? Avoid touching you in the market?" Simon guffawed at his own joke. I think he may have been understating it a bit when he said he didn't like them much. I think maybe he didn't like them a lot.

"He cared for my father when he was dying. Then he brought his body home so we could bury him and not have to wonder what happened to him."

Everyone was quiet for a moment; then Jesus quietly said, "Tell them the whole story. Like you told me."

I didn't want to. The story still hurt but since it was Jesus that asked, I told it.

"Not long after I came home from my little adventure in Corinth, my father was viciously attacked by robbers on the Jericho road outside Jerusalem. They not only took everything he was carrying, they liked his clothes, especially his nice robe, so they stripped him and stomped him as he lay in the road. Then they rolled him into a ditch and left him, unconscious and naked. We don't know how long he was there before Manasseh, the man I'm talking about, came by.

"I'm sure others passed by, it's a fairly busy road, but Manasseh is the one who stopped. He put him on his donkey and carried him to the closest inn where he tried his best to help him. In fact, he thought he was getting better, he was even able to sit up and talk, but one morning, just after Manasseh had talked to the innkeeper, telling him that he was leaving but he was to put my father's bill on his account, they came to his room and found him dead. He must have had some kind of internal injury they didn't know about. I am just glad that my father had the chance to tell him where he was from. My brother and I will forever be in Manasseh's debt."

I knew they were surprised to hear me talk about a Samaritan this way. Simon, our Zealot, had his lips pursed and his head was slightly shaking. Judas frowned and absent mindedly fingered the coins in our common purse. I pressed on, "Manasseh is one of the kindest and gentlest men I have ever known. He tended my father as best he could and had grown to care about him in the little time they had together. Manasseh was aghast that other people, probably good religious," I looked at Simon, "Samaritan-hating people, could have seen him and left him there to die, but he said my father told him, 'Don't think harshly of them. I was a mess and they had no idea how I had gotten there. Their fear was just too strong. It kept them from helping me.'

"Like I said, he lives near Jacob's well. If we go near there, I would like to visit him. Hopefully that wouldn't disturb his wife too much."

"Why would it disturb his wife?" Peter asked.

"She's had a very hard life and finds it hard to be around people. Not counting Manasseh she was married five times before she was with Manasseh." As soon as I said it, I wished I hadn't. It was none of their business and I knew they would jump to wrong conclusions.

"Five times! No, six times! How can a woman be married six times?" I don't remember who said that. It doesn't matter. They were all thinking it.

"I'll tell you how." My voice was shaking and I wanted to add "you son of bitch" but refrained. I'm pretty sure my tone let them know what I'd left off, and none of them dared not listen.

"Her father was a gambler, and he used her to pay off a debt when she was a child. After a year or so of abuse, that man got tired of her and let another man take her. The second man never got over her not being a virgin and divorced her. Then she met and married a kindly old man, but he died. His brother claimed her, thinking he could use her for profit, but she didn't cooperate, so he divorced her too. Number five thought she would at least be useful as a housekeeper, but he couldn't stand the scorn of the community, so he threw her out without warning one night after their evening meal, shouting so loudly the neighbors could hear it. Something about how she was such a bad cook she must be trying to poison him.

"Manasseh had known her since they were children, had secretly loved her, and it killed him to see her go through that life. He worked up the courage to ask her to marry him, but she told him that she was done with marriage. After a lot of coaxing and trust building, he took her into his house. He has tried to care for her, but her spirit is very damaged. Sometimes she stays inside for days, and sometimes she goes out just to pick a fight. He tells people she is his wife, and tells her that she should go where she wants to, when she wants to, with her head high. But I guess she is too wounded and will probably never be able to interact without running or striking out. I've seen animals like that. You want to help them, like Manasseh wants to help her, but they just won't let you.

"She is very religious in her own way. Prays a lot, ponders things. In fact, she taught herself to read and is very versed in their traditions but she never goes to their community worship. She even goes to the well at midday to avoid the other women."

I stopped and looked at them. I had never met her but she was my friend's wife. I think I would have fought them all, even James, if they made one more crack about all her husbands.

"What's her name?" asked Jesus.

"Photina."

Jesus slowly nodded his head, stroked his beard, stood up and said, "I think I would like a drink from Jacob's well. Let's go."

# Samaria's Well

OVER THE YEARS I had walked through Samaria a good bit without serious incident. Still, one couldn't help but feel a little uneasy. Let's just say hospitality wasn't a priority for Samaritans when it came to Jews. And, as it turns out, hospitality wasn't at all what we encountered when we were approaching Sychar, our destination village. Just on the outskirts we stopped and asked an innkeeper if he could put us up for a day or two. He was a big, stern looking man, gray at his temples with a long scar on his left cheek that I was guessing someone with a sharp object had given him in a fight. Perhaps I was led to guess that because he exhibited a willingness for violence when he started advancing toward us, laughing scornfully and waving his arms in a shooing fashion. Using some colorful language that referred to some of our family members, he told us to get off his property.

"Friend, we've walked several miles today. We're hungry, thirsty, and very tired. We'll pay a premium." This was Judas, our unofficial treasurer and negotiator. "We can see you don't have any guests today. Wouldn't some extra money be nice? Let us stay. I promise we won't be any trouble."

"You're already trouble! Get off my property! You are contaminating it!"

Judas started to say something else, but Jesus touched his arm and nodded toward the gate, it was time to let it go. Most of us just shrugged and walked off, but James, who was used to being the biggest, toughest guy in the room, glared back at the fellow, silently daring him to say one more word. I would not have liked to see those two tangle. It had been my experience that when heavyweights go at it, it can get gruesome in a hurry. The innkeeper didn't look intimidated by James at all, so I was thankful that Jesus kept herding us on our way.

When we gathered on the side of the road, in front of the inn, it took us a few minutes to make a plan for the evening. Since this was probably the only inn in town, it was decided that, since it didn't look like rain and the temperature was mild, it wouldn't be a big deal to sleep outside. Nothing unusual in that. We had certainly done it when it did look like rain and

39

the temperature wasn't mild. We could get water at the well, and, surely, we could find someone in the village to sell us some food.

The whole time we talked the fellow who owned the inn stood in his doorway with a look of disgust on his face. We ignored him for the most part, except for James who never took his eyes off of him.

When we started down the road, we were moving pretty slowly due to our weariness, so we hadn't gone far when I smelled smoke coming from behind us. When I turned around, I couldn't believe what I was seeing. I had heard about it but had never seen someone actually do it. The innkeeper had gathered some straw and, after quickly spreading it where we had been standing, set it on fire. He was burning our Jewish contamination off the land. "Fellows, I don't think he likes us." As if he heard me, the innkeeper pinched his nose and pretended to throw up. I'm guessing that was his way of saying it made him sick to be around us.

"That's it," said James. "That dog is about to get a lesson in hospitality." With that, James was charging back to the inn. John wasn't as easy to rile as James, but he always backed his brother, so he was right behind him.

Somehow Jesus got out front and stopped them. "Let's hold off on the thunder today boys. We didn't come to Samaria to start a riot. Take a breath. Let's give our rude friend something he isn't expecting, forgiveness." Then Jesus turned toward the Samaritan, held up a hand and said, just loud enough for the man to hear him, "We are truly sorry to have bothered you, friend. We are on our way now and won't bother you again." James and John weren't very pleased with that, but out of respect to Jesus they half waved and rejoined the group. In return for kindness shown, the innkeeper threw a rock that was fortunately wide to the right, and hollered something I couldn't understand. Jesus didn't seem to notice.

When we got to the well, we were disappointed to find that there was a rope for lowering buckets or whatever into the water but no buckets or whatever. All of us grumbled and felt hostility for a village that wouldn't leave something for travelers to draw water out of the well with. Even Jesus sighed and longingly looked down the well at his reflection in the water below.

"I guess we'll have to add a water pot to our shopping list," said Peter.

After we sat for a bit it was decided that most of the group would go into the little town and secure our supplies. Jesus said that he didn't feel like going and would stay, along with John and me at the well. As the rest walked off, Jesus called out, "No riots! You don't have to bark back every time you're barked at. I'm too tired to deal with any more excitement."

Since it was going to be a while before dinner, I slid off the rock I was sitting on, converted it from stool to headrest, and got ready for a little nap. Before I dozed off, I watched Jesus walk back over to the well and lose himself in thought as he stared into it. I wondered if he was thinking about Jacob and Joseph, our patriarchs, and their time at this same spot hundreds of years ago, or maybe he was simply thinking about how good some cool, well water would taste right after walking several miles on a warm morning.

It didn't feel like I had been asleep very long, but I was certainly sleeping hard when John nudged me and whispered, "Here comes someone, a lone woman." That was unusual and dimly rang a bell in my sleepy brain, but I was distracted by the fact that she kept approaching even though she saw three strange men lounging where she was headed.

At first I thought this must be because of boldness and confidence, but, when she got closer, I saw that she was coming at us more like a feral cat whose thirst was more powerful than her fear. I thought about shutting my eyes again and acting like I didn't know she was there. Maybe that would make her feel safer. I couldn't shake the feeling that something should be clicking for me right then, my tiredness and thirst just wouldn't let me put all the pieces together.

She was relatively small in stature and gave the impression that she was doing everything in her power to make herself smaller. Every move she made signaled distress, and her eyes darted from Jesus to John to me and back to Jesus. I didn't know what would happen if one of us moved suddenly. Would she have run away or would she have picked up a stone and tried to bash us?

Nobody said anything as she slowly tied the rope around the water pot and lowered it into the well. When she pulled it up, some of the clear, up to now inaccessible, water spilled onto the ground. I remember thinking to myself, that would have tasted pretty good. Jesus must have thought the same thing because he asked her, "Do you think I could have a drink of that?" and we got our answer as to whether she would have been more inclined to run or bash.

"Where do you get off talking to me, man!? A woman can't come to the well for water without strange men accosting her? Leave me alone!" She didn't look as small as she had a moment earlier. Both her hands were balled into fists, and I got the impression that it wasn't from stress so much as a readiness to use them.

Jesus surprised all of us when he said, "Photina, we have a common friend. I only wanted some water and to talk to you for a little while." Photina! Of course! That was the reason Jesus had stayed at the well with John and me when the others went for food.

"I told you to leave me alone," she snarled, "I don't know how you know my name, but if you come closer to me I'll give you a drink of water, pot and all to the side of your head. If you don't leave me alone, I'll go tell my husband and brother that there are a couple Jews here that don't know they aren't supposed to talk to Samaritan women."

"Photina, I said we have a common friend. As strange as it sounds, I'm actually here to see you. I'm told you are very religious." He smiled, raised one eyebrow as he looked at her water pot and said, "I know my saying I was waiting on you sounds very odd. I'm sorry. I'm just tired, thirsty, and not sure what to say. You may be interested in what I have to say."

"How could a traveling beggar, excuse me a very religious beggar, a Jewish prophet," pretty sure she was being sarcastic, "possibly have anything to say that I would find interesting? You can't even get your own water." She looked at the three of us and laughed at us and our predicament. Then she said, "I mean it. My husband is visiting my brother at his inn just up the road. They can be here in a few minutes and make you wish you'd never spoken to me."

Great, I thought. Our inner keeper buddy again. But now I was fully awake and jumped in. "Photina, I am the mutual friend he's talking about, sort of. We haven't met, but I know your husband, Manasseh. He was very kind to my family a few years ago, and I would love to see him again. We certainly don't want any trouble, but I wish you would tell him I'm here." I wanted to say, and if you could not mention us to your brother, that'd be great, but I left that part out.

She was taken back a little as she realized we not only knew her name but I knew Manasseh as well. I pressed on. "Manasseh brought my father home to my brother and me so we could bury him. He is one of the most gracious people I have ever known. Your brother makes me nervous, but I would really like to see Manasseh."

She softened a little, even hinted at a smile when I mentioned her brother. "I'll go get him. I know who you are. Manasseh told me about your family. He'll be glad to see you." She then looked at Jesus and said, "I'll leave my pot. Help yourself." As she headed for the inn, the three of us headed for the water. It was as good as we had imagined, if not better.

When the others returned they were flabbergasted to find six of us sitting in a circle, talking while Manasseh and I renewed acquaintances. He asked all kinds of questions about the farm and was sorry to hear that my brother and I were estranged. He was genuinely glad to see me as I was also glad to see him. Photina and her brother, whose name was Hosea, seemed incredulous that Jews and Samaritans could actually like each other. Hosea did manage to almost apologize for his earlier greeting. Something about having a bad day, having always had a temper that was too quick, some bad experiences with Jewish boarders in the past . . . never quite got around to saying that he was sorry, but he got closer than I ever thought he would. Close enough for Jesus.

Manasseh announced that we would all stay at his brother-in-law's inn that night. Before the innkeeper could object, Manasseh said that he would cover the expense. It wasn't lost on me that this was not only generous, but it made Manasseh the customer, so now we couldn't be turned away. Jesus smiled in Hosea's direction and said that we would add whatever the others had purchased in town to supper. I could tell Jesus was starting to think banquet. The rest of us slowly got on board, in varying but growing degrees.

Somehow it turned into a banquet indeed. Every time we added something from our supplies to the table the innkeeper would add something of his own. It turned into a feast and as bread and wine were passed, defensiveness, prejudices, and walls began to come down.

I would have thought it impossible, but James actually made a new friend. It started when he and Hosea both reached for the same lamb's leg, their hands grabbing it at exactly the same time. Neither would let go, in fact, their grips got tighter. The table got quiet as we all nervously watched to see what would happen. After what seemed like several seconds, though it probably wasn't more than four or five, Jesus said, "Not exactly what I was thinking about for tonight's entertainment but it should be fun to watch a little tug of war." We took a collective breath, James and Hosea seemed to loosen their clench a little, then Peter guffawed and the rest of the table joined in. The combatants didn't let go immediately, but, after a couple of nudges and John picking up another leg and playfully taking turns offering it to them, they blushed a little and joined in the laughter. Later that night James and Hosea were seen sitting outside, laughing and swapping stories about who knows what.

Before we left the table Matthew said he had a song he wanted to sing for us. It was about Jacob and his wrestling with the mysterious stranger all night. He said he picked that song because we were close to the well named after Jacob, but also because it seemed to him that we had been doing a little internal wrestling of our own. We were all headed toward a new morning, changed in a good way, like Jacob who got his new name, Israel, after his wrestling match. Jesus loved it.

While James and Hosea swapped back slaps, Jesus and Photina had their conversation. I didn't hear all of it but it was long and heartfelt. I could tell that she was telling him her life's story, and I knew that she knew that she was being heard with deep empathy and without any judgment. When I saw that Jesus was giving her "the look," I grinned and nudged Matthew. All of us had experienced our version of that conversation and gotten that look. I heard Jesus say, "You must be one of the strongest people I've ever met."

When I was sure they weren't talking about private things anymore, I joined them and listened as they moved into theological things. She had amazing depth, and, even though they were from different traditions, she and Jesus brought each other to life with insights and questions. She was not only well-read and thoughtful in her own religion, it was obvious that she had read our law and prophets as well. Both brought thoughts to the conversation that the other appreciated.

One of the things I remember is when they were talking about where the best place to worship was. Samaritans believe their mountain is God's throne and of course Jews believe that the temple in Jerusalem is the holiest of places. Jesus's take on that was that he was afraid people could be tempted to put too much emphasis on the place. He said that, if we weren't careful, it would be like putting God in a box, and we could start reverencing the place and the tradition more than we actually worshiped God. He said that we could and should worship everywhere, that our very bodies could be thought of as holy places. He added that his goal was to worship with all his heart and to worship honestly. He said that many seem to slip into superstition, like God and religious things were good luck charms. She took in what he said, nodded her head and said, "Yes. I've always thought that myself."

# Back in Capernaum

WE STAYED AT HOSEA'S inn three more nights, each night building on the previous as the number of people in attendance grew and the amount of food and wine multiplied even more. Word spread quickly through the small village that Photina was a changed woman. People were coming to see her and the man that had brought the new Photina out.

It was good to see old wounds begin to heal between the town's people and Photina. It was also amazing to see Jesus teach Samaritans about the love of God and watch them receive it with joy. When it was time to continue our journey, I had the impression that Jesus could have started a synagogue in Sychar, and everyone in town would have attended. But the inevitable morning came when we heard Jesus's summons, "Time to go," and we began our goodbyes.

Photina had truly been transformed. Her inner confidence and trust toward others radiated from her, but she hated to see Jesus go. She shared her fear with him that the new way may not last. She was pretty scared and told him that she had been the old Photina for a long time. She realized that smiling for four days during a party and doing life were two different things.

Jesus took both her hands in his, gave her that Jesus look one more time, and said that she would be fine. She could trust herself and God to show her the way in her new life, day by day. Of course there would be hard days, but they wouldn't last—keep going. Just like something Jesus would say.

James and Hosea gave each other a strong, manly (of course), embrace, and James said, "Go with God, my Samaritan friend." Not something I could imagine James saying four days earlier.

As we made our way out of Samaritan territory, I thought about the conversation we had had when we were deciding if we would go through Samaria. It occurred to me that Photina wasn't the only one that had been changed in Sychar. Hang around with Jesus and the circle just keeps getting wider and wider. Your circle of friends and the circle that tries to contain your heart.

We got back to Capernaum just before the sunset that would begin Sabbath time. Jesus and Peter went to Peter's house where Mary was staying with Peter's wife and mother-in-law. The rest of us went to Matthew's house and were warmly greeted by Julius, his partner who had been tending the business in Matthew's absence. Everyone was tired from a few days of walking steadily, and not long after our light supper snoring filled the house.

I don't think anyone was ready to wake up when Matthew called us for breakfast, but, knowing we were headed to worship at Capernaum's synagogue where we would see Nathaniel and Leah got us going, even put smiles on our faces. Anticipation of his warm greeting and her infectious laugh did more to wake us up than the smell of roasting fish and baking bread.

We weren't disappointed. We met Jesus and the folks from Peter's house on the street just before we got to the synagogue, and we heard Nathaniel and his daughter before we saw them. "Look who's back!" called Nathaniel and "It's Jesus!" squealed Leah. She couldn't be contained. She ran down the street into Jesus arms and gave him a big hug, then she went around hugging each of us, calling us by name, except Peter whom she called "Uncle."

"Jesus! Peter! James! John! Judas! Matthew! Andrew!" Nathaniel made each one of us feel like it would have been a huge disappointment if we hadn't come to worship. "Jesus, I had a reading planned, but, now that you are here, I can't wait to hear what you will share."

"Not this morning, my friend. I'm looking forward to listening to you. I need a good word, a good Nathaniel-word today."

They went back and forth a couple of times, but Jesus was insistent.

When we walked through the door, I was more than a little surprised that Simon wasn't there. In fact, a few of his closest friends were absent as well. Like I said, it was surprising but certainly not disappointing. I wasn't going to miss him.

We took our places, and the service started. To be honest, Nathaniel wasn't the most eloquent speaker, but what he lacked in eloquence he made up for in sincerity and practicality. He made the scripture easy to apply in real life. Show hospitality, treat others as if they were visiting angels, trust God's love, and pray from your heart. That was pretty much Nathaniel's message Sabbath after Sabbath, but it was so sincere and authentically lived by Nathaniel it always revived the soul.

After the closing prayers, we were standing on the synagogue porch telling Nathaniel about our adventures in Samaria when Simon did finally show up. The smirk on his face made me uneasy as I watched him march through the small crowd, directly to Jesus. There were a few people behind him, and there seemed to be some pushing and shoving going on but Simon demanded our attention.

"Jesus! I heard you were back in town and I thought you'd want to see how effective your mushy teaching is." He could barely contain himself. "I told you there had to be lines between good and bad. If you let people think that God loves them no matter what, everything would fall apart." He turned toward his friends, "Bring her here. Let's show Jesus how one of his favorite followers turned out!"

We could hear quiet sobs, "No, no please," as two men pulled a woman toward Simon. When they got her to him, he shoved her toward Jesus, making her lose her balance and fall to her hands and knees. It was Rachel. My heart sank, James tensed and stood like a lion ready to strike, Judas shook his head in disappointment, Peter looked confused, and a tear came to Jesus's eye as he knelt beside Rachel. She had no jewelry at all. She loved jewelry, and I had never seen her without lots of it. I looked over her accusers for signs of a new ring.

"Jesus, we caught your friend in the act of adultery. Thought you'd want to know!" Simon was grinning like he'd just won some kind of high stakes game. But this wasn't a game. It was a woman's life. He had broken her and was glad to do it.

"What are you doing, Simon?" It was Nathaniel. "We just finished Sabbath worship. My little girl is here. What's wrong with you?"

"What's wrong with me? I'm trying to show you what's wrong with Jesus and the milk-toast teaching you and he offer these gullible sheep." He sneered and mockingly said, "'Treat others like you want to be treated and everything will be fine.' Ha!" He looked down at Leah and said, "Nathaniel, if you don't listen to me, your daughter will be just like this woman! I'm glad your girl is here. She needs to see her future if she doesn't take scripture seriously!"

"Nathaniel, take Leah and go home. We'll talk later. It'll be okay," said Jesus. He looked at Leah, because he was kneeling, they were eye to eye. "We'll talk later, sweet girl. See you soon."

Her face was a mass of confusion, her eyes were filling and her lower lip was trembling, "Jesus, what's going on? Why are they being so mean to her?"

"It's okay. We'll talk about it later. Go with your father."

A couple of Simon's gang stepped toward Nathaniel but Simon said, "Let them go. If God's will is to be done here today, it's probably best that the girl isn't here. She'll remember though, and one day she'll thank us."

As Nathaniel and Leah walked off Jesus asked, "Who was Rachel with?"

"Doesn't matter. It wasn't anyone gullible enough to believe the drivel you try to get people to believe, so he doesn't need the lesson this woman needs." I noticed that one of the young men toward the back of the crowd looked uneasy and was being very careful not to meet Jesus's eyes. Jesus noticed him too.

"Simon, you set her up. Are you willing to hurt her just to get to me?"

"I don't have any idea what you are talking about, but I do know what the scripture says. 'Thou shall not commit adultery' and 'anyone caught in adultery is to be stoned to death.' That's God's word. That's what needs to be done here and we're going to do it. No one in this town will blame us, and no one will report us to the Romans for taking the law into our own hands. It's a religious matter, and we are in the right." Rachel continued her muffled sobbing and the young man toward the back of the crowd disappeared.

Jesus continued to kneel in front of Rachel and tried to look into her face, but she would have none of it. He paused for a moment, rubbing his hand across the earth, then he picked up a stone a little larger than an egg and said, "Okay, if you all are so determined to stone a sinner today, how about this. The one here that is without sin—throw the first stone. Here it is, who wants it?" Then he opened his hand and held the stone out toward the crowd.

Simon snatched it and gripped it like he would hurl it in the next moment. His eyes focused on Rachel's head like it was a target, but before he threw, he paused and looked around to see what the others were doing. They weren't doing anything.

Simon gave Rachel's head another look, his arm moved back slightly, ready to throw but he stopped and looked at his supporters again. Reuben, an old man that had grown up going to that very synagogue, sighed deeply, looked at Simon, shook his head and walked off. A couple of more followed him. No one picked up a stone.

Simon's vein was showing again. "Damn you Jesus," and he suddenly threw the rock at Jesus, who twisted his body just in time for it to hit with a thud in his side. Mary gasped. I thought a hit like that would leave a bad mark, perhaps crack a rib. Jesus barely flinched, and kept looking at Simon, no fear showing.

"Jesus, I want to tell you something, and, for the first time, you better listen." He looked at Mary and said, "You better make sure he hears me." Back to Jesus, "Passover is coming, and, if I were you, I wouldn't go to Jerusalem this year. I've been giving the leaders there reports on you. If you come to Jerusalem this year, you'll never leave. You hear me, Jesus? A sinner will die if you come to Jerusalem, and it will be you. You hear me Jesus?"

"I hear you, Simon. I hear you. I think you're done here. Leave us alone." With that, Simon turned and left, as did the few of his companions that were still there.

Jesus reached to take Rachel's hand, but she refused, snatching it away. She looked at the ground for a moment, took a deep breath, slowly stood, and shook her hair back. She absent-mindedly put her hand where a necklace should have been, looked at the sky, and said to the still kneeling Jesus, "Well, I guess we see what I truly am now don't we?"

"What's that, Rachel?"

"You know!"

"I do know," he said as he stood. "I know Simon doesn't, and I'm not sure you do." Finally, she met his eyes with her eyes. They held each other's gaze for several seconds, and Jesus said, "I'm sorry."

"You're sorry? Jesus, you spent time with me, taught me things about God I could barely believe. You taught me to pray, called me a friend, and you leave town for a few days and this . . . this is what I become. This is who I am. What an idiot."

"Rachel, I don't know what you are thinking right now when you say, 'this is who I am,' and please, please don't call yourself an idiot. Again, people like Simon don't have a clue who you really are. They don't even know what they are. If there is something inside you that is telling you that Simon is right, he's not. Don't listen. I know who you are, and I'm telling you now, you are God's beloved child."

"God's child?" She said incredulously and started weeping. "God's child? I wish. I thought maybe . . . but, obviously . . . not even close! How can you say that?"

"Rachel," he got her attention again. "Rachel, I have a question for you. Let's say it's ten years from now and Leah is standing where you are."

"She wouldn't!"

"Let's say she is. No one plans to be thrown in the dirt and condemned by religious bullies. Let's say she is. Would she still be Nathaniel's child? Would he love her, bring her home, care for her hurts, and help her grow from her pain?"

"Of course he would. Everyone knows how much he loves that little girl."

"Rachel, Nathaniel is not greater than God. His love isn't greater than God's. Love like he has for Leah is supposed to show us God's love for us.

"Take this pain you are feeling today and don't let it condemn you. Let it push you into God's presence, not away from it. Heal. Grow. Be wiser and stronger. You will."

"If I don't, will you throw the stone next time? If anyone here could, by your standards, it would be you. If I do this again next week and the week after and the week after, will you throw the stone, Jesus? There has to be a line. When will you throw it, Jesus?"

The hurt on Jesus's face was evident. "Rachel. That will never happen."

And then, right on time if you will, Mary walked up to Rachel, tenderly wiped the tears from her eyes with her own sleeve, put her arm around her, and led her down the hill to Peter's house.

# The Decision

THAT EVENING WE ATE at Peter's. All of us were there including Mary and Rachel. They were sitting side by side, just as they had been all afternoon as they talked in a nearby garden.

"Well, I guess we won't be going to Jerusalem for Passover this year," said Peter as if the decision had already been made, because, in his mind, it had. It certainly seemed to me like there should be no question as to whether we went to Jerusalem or not. We had all heard Simon's threat, and most of us had seen the ugly bruise on Jesus's side when Peter's mother-in-law checked his ribs and bandaged him up. Simon had proven he could be violent.

"I don't know, Peter. I haven't decided," said Jesus. "I'm not sure what I should do. I'm going to pray about it. I'd like it if the rest of you would as well."

"Pray about it?!" Peter was stunned. "What's to pray about? You heard Simon. You think he was joking? He didn't sound like he was joking to me! That bruise on your side feel like a joke?"

Everyone was quiet for a moment as Peter tried, without much success, to calm himself. He took a deep breath and started again, "Think about it, Jesus, here in Capernaum everyone knows you and loves you. That helps keep Simon in check, but even here he roughs up Rachel and throws a rock into your side. What would have happened if that thing had hit you in the head?" He was starting to talk faster and leaned toward Jesus. "Now think about what it'd be like in Jerusalem. There are hundreds like Simon there, and he's already been turning them against you. They don't know you in Jerusalem. You're just some traveling prophet from Galilee they've heard of. Half what they've heard is not right. It's crazy to even consider. Jesus, there's nothing to pray about, talk about, or think about. We aren't going to Jerusalem."

"Peter, I haven't decided. I'm going to pray about it, and I'll let you know. I can't let fear make the decision for me. A big part of me feels like I need to go. To make a statement, to not let fear overcome. I don't know. There will be thousands of people there, many from all over the world. Maybe I need to go and spend some time talking to people on the teaching steps at the temple. Maybe I can clear up some of the things that are being said about me. Yes, I think it may be a good time to go to Jerusalem. Simon will certainly have people talking about me and what I teach. It could actually be a good opportunity to share exactly what I'm saying."

For some reason Judas caught my eye. He was nodding his head in agreement.

Peter started back, "Okay, I get that you can't let fear dictate your actions, and it's good to help people understand things, but you can't be stupid either!" His emotions were out of control again. With each word his voice got louder and more strained.

"Enough!" Now Jesus's voice was as strained as Peter's. He glared at Peter and said, "You sound like someone who doesn't believe God is involved!" He shouted that part, but then he slowly and clearly said, "I will seek to follow God's will. I will not listen to fear or to you when you are talking like this, even if you think you are making sense. You haven't prayed about it for a second. Again, enough!" His voice rose again on the last two words, and he looked around at the rest of us to see if we had anything to say. I could hear a cart go by the house as we sat without uttering a word. None of us were going to jump into that. It was the most agitated I ever saw Jesus get with one of us. Actually, he was mad at all of us. He knew we agreed with Peter.

Mary picked up a loaf of bread, broke off a portion and passed it to Rachel without a word. Our normally lively conversation around the table wasn't to be that night. Things stayed pretty quiet the rest of the evening.

The next morning I made a point of rising early because I knew Jesus would. It was going to be the most important prayer time yet, and I wanted to be there. I thought maybe he would want someone to sit with him as he prayed. I knew he would be seeking direction on Jerusalem. Maybe he would need an ear. I wasn't sure what I could say, but I could listen. I don't know if he welcomed my tagging along, but he allowed it.

There was no moon that night and not a hint of dawn when we left the house, but, with a single torch, we found our way to where Mary and Rachel had sat the day before. We sat together for a few minutes. He shared with me that his night had been restless. "I was thinking about Jerusalem and its history. It's a holy place, the city of God. So much has happened there that is wonderful and sacred. But, so much has happened there that is awful. So many prophets have been killed by people who thought they were doing God a favor. People like Simon."

I nodded and said, "Yes there has. There's been a lot of bad stuff. Maybe more than any place in the world. It doesn't seem like there's ever been a time, anywhere, when someone wasn't willing to kill folks who disagreed with them."

"So many prophets tried to share about justice and forgiveness. Trying to do what was loving, trying to speak for those who had no voice, no power, suffering . . . crying out. Killed . . . trying to be true to God . . ." His voice trailed off. I didn't like how this was going.

He told me that he wanted to have some time alone and asked me to remain where we were sitting while he went to a large rock about a hundred feet away.

The day began to dawn, and I extinguished the torch. From where I sat, I could see Jesus but I couldn't understand what he was saying. Even without hearing the words, I could tell that his stress was almost unbearable. He was pouring himself out. Two doves landed just the other side of the rock. Almost like they were listening in.

It was at least an hour, probably longer. Sometimes Jesus would hold his hands out with his palms up. Sometimes he would run them through his hair and lift his strained face toward the sky. As the sun got higher and the day became brighter, I could see that he was sweating a good bit. I remember that because I wasn't. It was actually kind of chilly.

Finally, I heard him say, firmly and as clearly as if he were right beside me, "Amen. Your will be done." He got up and, as he walked back toward me, his face looked different than I had ever seen it. It was a look of determination, a strong look. I didn't see any of the joy that was usually apparent, and I didn't see any of the fear that one would expect to see on the face of someone that had just decided to walk into mortal danger. Just determination, he had made his decision.

At breakfast, the quietness from the night before remained. Peter didn't bother to pretend to be eating. No one wanted a repeat of the scene from last night's supper, but everyone knew an announcement was coming, and I think everyone could tell from the way Jesus looked and acted what it would be.

When he was ready, Jesus put his bread down and waited for everyone's attention. All of us stopped eating and looked at him—except Mary. She stared down at the food that she hadn't touched, hadn't even pushed around. Tears were forming in her eyes, about to start down her face.

"I'm going to Jerusalem for Passover." That's all he said. He didn't say anything about doing a lot of praying, a lot of thinking, and nothing along the lines of: I know you all don't want me to. Just an announcement.

No one said a word. I'm not even sure anyone was breathing. It was like we all exhaled and forgot for a few moments to inhale. Jesus had made his decision, and now we all had one to make. There was no doubt that Simon and his kind would be perfectly willing to throw a rock at us as well. It was easy to imagine that if Simon intended to make good on his threat, it would require a good bit of courage to be seen as a follower of Jesus.

We did start breathing again, but for a solid minute no one spoke. The only noise was an occasional deep sigh and a happily cawing hooded crow near the door that apparently had no idea how inappropriate he was being. I pressed my fist against my forehead and wished I would wake up. I looked at Mary. Her tears were dripping, her lips were pursed, but she was silent.

Someone finally spoke. "Well, if you're going to Jerusalem, I'm going with you," it was Rachel. Mary was still crying, but she looked up and caught Rachel's eye. Through the fear and pain, I saw a slight smile and a deeply grateful nod. Mary was going too. We all were going.

It was two days before we started. When we got going it wasn't with a Jesus I had seen before. He was quiet, very quiet. He mostly walked by himself. Sometimes he was in the lead, but, just as often, he was a good bit behind us.

It wasn't like he was dragging. His stride remained steady, and he kept the determined look I had seen in the garden, but his mood was heavy.

As we walked, he not only didn't have much to say to us, his traveling companions, he didn't interact with people along the way either. Occasionally, he would stop and talk to a beggar, or, if he noticed someone that was obviously in pain at one of the inns where we stayed, he would try to comfort them, but mostly he just walked. We went to sleep early, got up early, and walked. More like a march than a pilgrimage to a holy city for a sacred day.

We got to our destination a week before Passover. We spent our last Sabbath before entering the city with Martha and her family in Bethany, so it was the first day of the week when we stood at the top of the Mount of Olives and looked across the valley at the temple and the holy city that surrounded it: the pride of Judaism. It was a magnificent view. One wondered how humans could have built such a structure. Massive stones, one on top of the other. Beautiful. Magnificent. Awesome. God's house.

We paused there for a good while, each of us in our own thoughts. Then Jesus offered one of the saddest prayers I've ever heard. He wasn't sad for himself; he was sad for Jerusalem and the people he knew would be there opposing him. His voice choked when he lamented that it is often the most religious people that have the most trouble seeing the truth and sharing love. When he was through with the prayer, he started down the mountainside and we followed.

As we made our way, somehow the beauty of the temple, the bustle of the city, and the spirit of the upcoming holy day temporarily quieted our fear and lifted our spirits. Matthew, the most musical one in our group, began to sing one of the psalms, "Lift up your heads you gates, the king of glory will come in," and one by one we all joined in, even Jesus.

I guess twenty or so people marching into town while singing draws attention because soon several children ran up and joined the festivity. That attracted even more people, and, before we reached the bottom of the mountain and began our ascent into the city proper, we had a small parade. Disciples, children, shop owners, beggars, people of the street, and folks just wondering what was going on; we were quite a crowd.

James and John found a donkey and decided no one would mind if they borrowed it. James grabbed Jesus and put him on it, and now Jesus was the grand marshal. When that happened, our love for Jesus, our fear for his life, and our sadness over Jerusalem's poor track record when faced with love and truth, changed our singing to shouts of "Hosanna, God save!" The people who knew it was the teacher from Galilee entering the city and the people who had no idea who we were but thought "God save" was a good thing to shout all joined us. By the time we reached the teaching steps of the temple, to be honest, we were a little out of control, border line rowdy.

When we arrived, I couldn't believe my eyes. There he was, bright yellow and red, long-sleeved robe, oversized phylacteries. It was Simon. He was about half way up the steps, scowling at us. Everyone knew the parade had reached its end, and, when folks quieted down enough for him to be heard, Simon shouted down at us, "Again Jesus, you show that you have no respect for what's holy. Who are these people you've brought to God's house? You don't even know them. No telling when was the last time most of them got this close to the Temple. Do they even know where the ceremonial baths are? Look at them, most don't even know what a bath is. Tell them to be quiet!"

Jesus stared back for a couple of seconds, sighed, and said, "Simon, every one of them is a child of God, calling for God to save the people. That's the cry of every heart, the cry of everything that is, even the rocks. Every stone of this great building cries out, 'God save.' How can you find anything wrong with that? I am not going to tell a single one of them to hush. Even if I tried, creation's cry for healing would go on."

"We'll talk later Jesus," Simon snarled, "You are going to find out that there are many who think of you as I do. I think you are going to regret coming. I told you that you would." With that he turned and walked up the steps to the courtyard. Several others that I hadn't noticed in all the commotion followed him. The party was over. The dread and wondering if we should have come had returned.

# Jesus Loses It

THE NEXT MORNING, JUST as he said he would be, Jesus was sitting on the teaching steps making conversation with any who were interested. I think Simon's greeting had actually backfired. His less than friendly reception had caused a good bit of curiosity, and quite a crowd gathered around to hear what this man who was causing such a stir had to say.

I had never heard Jesus's teaching be more focused and clear than it was that morning. He seemed to feel an urgency to get the heart of his message out there. The questions, especially from those who were genuinely seeking understanding invigorated him.

He talked about how the kingdom of God is hidden but always active in our lives. He shared that even the smallest act of kindness had value; plus, he was pretty critical of those not living a lifestyle that is consistent with what they professed. It was clear, simple, and life changing for those who caught what he was saying.

After about an hour, Matthew nudged me in the side and directed my attention to the top of the steps. Simon, along with a few priestly looking men, was headed our way. I expected a blow up and was very surprised by Simon's tone when he greeted us.

"Good morning, Jesus! I see you are already hard at work this morning, spreading your message. Good, that's good.

"I would like to apologize for the way I spoke yesterday. Last night I realized that you had done the right thing coming here as it will give us a chance to talk with you and ask some questions while our best teachers and respected leaders are listening. I was wondering if I could join in the conversation and ask you some questions about what you believe. I know an honest teacher like yourself wouldn't mind our having a little dialogue, while everyone listens in."

None of us were having this new Simon, especially since it didn't occur to him that he was interrupting as he made his way to the front of the crowd. Jesus said nothing, but he did force a smile as Simon took his position.

"Good," said Simon. "I know that you have some Zealots in your group. I was wondering how you felt about paying taxes to Rome. It's true you have a former tax collector in the group as well, but he seems to have resigned his post. Is it your position that we should pay our taxes or not?"

That was a masterful question. In just a couple of sentences Simon had driven a wedge in our gathering. Zealots versus Roman sympathizers, not to mention the three soldiers that had quietly taken position at the bottom of the steps. It occurred to me that their presence was prearranged. There was no answer to Simon's question that wouldn't drive some people away, and there was at least one answer that could lead to Jesus's arrest there and then for sedition.

Jesus thought for a second and then said, "Simon, I think everyone here is aware that you are trying to trap me and find some reason to have me arrested. I'm going to play along for a bit, but first let me make this very clear to those who may be feeling ill feelings toward anyone here this morning. I tell you with all my heart that God loves and welcomes everyone that can hear my voice. Zealots, tax collectors, priests, shop keepers, soldiers, people of the street, and people who sleep in luxury, all are beloved and invited to walk in the way I am sharing this morning. If you don't hear anything else I say today, hear that.

"Now. Your question. Well done. Do you happen to have a coin on you?" Simon's face was taking on some color, but he reached into his purse and pulled out a Roman coin. "Whose image is on that coin, Simon?"

Simon looked a little puzzled because we all knew the image of Caesar was on the coin, but he answered, "Caesar's."

"Then why don't we just give Caesar what's his, but, at the same time, and more importantly, give God what is God's."

Simon looked confused for a bit, but then he ruefully smiled. "Jesus, you are nothing if not clever. You are saying that our coins have Caesar's image on them and are part of his kingdom, but it's your belief that everyone here has God's image on them so we give ourselves to God."

"Yes. Thank you, Simon."

"Oh, I get it, and I think my next questions will show the danger of what you are saying, so thank you for being so clear.

"First, let's see if we agree on something. What would you say is the greatest of all commands?" Even I knew this one.

"You shall love the Lord your God with all your heart, mind, soul, and strength." said Jesus. He paused and then added, "And inseparable from that is this, 'love your neighbor as yourself.'"

"Would you expand on that, Jesus?" Simon was obviously setting another trap, and Jesus had stopped forcing his smile.

"It's pretty straightforward, Simon. Our call is to love the Lord with everything we have, in all the ways we can. We do this by loving our neighbors as if they are actually a part of our self. The best way to do this is to do for others as you would have them do for you. Treat every elder as you want people to treat your parents. Treat every child as you want people to treat your children. Respect every woman and man as you would want people to respect your sisters and brothers, especially those who are suffering and in need—the ones who are being overlooked."

That was pretty much Jesus in a nutshell, but Simon wasn't through, and, judging by the look on his face, he thought he had Jesus right where he wanted him. "You keep saying 'every' and 'all.' Surely there is a distinction. God loves righteousness and despises sin. Don't you think that our priority needs to be towards God's people? Don't you think some of the people that you say we should respect are suffering because they are getting what they deserve?"

I looked at Jesus, and the energy that I had seen before was waning. Simon seemed to be wearing him down. He was starting to look irritated. I hoped he could contain himself. Surely, he would. He barely flinched when Simon creamed him with that stone.

"Simon, all people are God's people, and, in a very real way, we are all part of the same family. We are all one, a part of one another. We are all created by God, we all share this world, we all love, and we all need love."

"Okay Jesus, let's clear it up once and for all. You say 'love your neighbor' and I agree. Who is our neighbor?"

Jesus paused and looked at me and held my eye for a moment. It was like he was giving me some kind of warning or a heads up as to what was about to come. Simon wanted to clear it up? I had a feeling we were about to clear it up.

"Simon, there was once a man who had business that required him to leave home abruptly and travel alone on the road not far from here. In spite of the promise of Roman protection, he was attacked by robbers. He was beaten almost to death, robbed of everything he had, even his clothes, and left on the side of the road to die. As he lay there bleeding out, several people came by. Many were religious people, teachers and leaders in the Temple, but they didn't stop. Some even crossed over to the other side of the road so they wouldn't see the gore or hear his moans."

When he talked about Roman protection, he looked at the three soldiers, when he mentioned the religious people his gaze took in the crowd all around us, and when he got to the leaders of the Temple his eyes locked with Simon's.

"When he was almost dead, a Samaritan approached." I shut my eyes but I could feel the tension in the crowd as Jesus, standing on Jerusalem's Temple steps, brought a Samaritan into his story. "This Samaritan was moved by the poor man's suffering. He too had places to be, important things to take care of—and he was in unfriendly territory—but he stopped. He applied aid to the man's body, dressed him, and took him to shelter at a nearby inn. He told the innkeeper to spare no expense in caring for the man and to please secure the best doctor available. He said that he would bear all cost."

Jesus ended the story there and paused for a few seconds as he looked over the crowd again. Then he said, "Simon, of all the people in the story, which one treated the man like he would want to be treated if he were the one in the ditch? Which one knew that the man on the side of the road was also a part of the human family? Which one was the neighbor?"

Simon's face was red and his vein was showing again. He wouldn't answer. He turned and walked away.

"Which one Simon!?" Jesus shouted after him. "Which one!? You won't answer because you know you would have to change your thinking, and you are too afraid, too attached to your belief to change! You're afraid Simon! You love praise and position and possessions more than God! Which one, Simon?"

Peter walked over and took Jesus by the arm, but he shook free. "Let me go, Peter! I've had it! I'm tired. I'm so tired of all this!" Now he wasn't talking to Simon or Peter, he was just shouting. "This place is supposed to be a house of prayer for all people! This building is supposed to be the place where we come together and worship the one who made us! When we come here, we are supposed to remember who we are! Lord, God! It's been taken over by people who love themselves more than anything. It's been taken over by people who are willing to hurt and destroy others to protect their status! Lord, God! I've had it!"

With that he stormed down the steps, past the soldiers, and over to one of the tables that were set up to exchange foreign coins for temple coins so pilgrims could buy their sacrifices. Behind the table, the poor money changer's eyes grew as big as saucers as Jesus came at him. Jesus grabbed the table, literally roared, and flung it as far as he could. Coins went everywhere, but no one moved. No one except the soldiers. The one in the lead came at Jesus with a small whip with several tails. He hit Jesus across the back and ordered him to pick up the money and put the table back in its place.

Jesus spun around, grabbed the soldier's wrist and snatched the whip from him. He raised it like he was about to beat the stunned soldier, but shoved him back into the other two and shouted. "No more today! No more business today! No more stealing and lying today!" He looked at the soldiers and shouted at them, "No more whipping today!" and threw the whip all the way to the top of the steps. The whip was still bouncing when Jesus turned and walked through the stunned crowd that was parting before him.

I turned back and looked up the steps. Simon was standing there, actually smiling. Judas was standing next to him, trying to get his attention. I went quickly up the stairs, wanting to find out what Judas was doing up there. By the time I reached them Simon was telling Judas, "I think you're right, Judas. Perhaps we could talk some more but not here. It's too tense right now and the crowd is restless. If you could take me to where you are camped, perhaps a conversation in the quiet of night."

I got Judas's attention and shook my head no. Judas held up his hand and said, "Let me think about it. I just want everyone to see that we are all on the same side here. We all want to see Israel restored to greatness. We're just misunderstanding each other."

Simon rubbed his beard with one hand and put the other on Judas's shoulder, "Of course, friend. That's what we all want. You don't have to be concerned. If Jesus is on God's side, nothing can stop him. There's nothing to fear, no harm will come to him."

My heart sank. What was Judas doing?

# Arrested

THE REST OF THE week went by without any shouting or thrown tables, but, when we reached Passover, none of us expected to make it out of the city without incident. We learned later that the Temple leaders had held several meetings to discuss how to capture Jesus without causing a riot and put an end to his teaching once and for all. We also learned that Judas had been present at at least one of those meetings, though I never believed that he realized what they actually had in mind. I think only a handful of those involved were filled with perverse religious hatred. Most were either simply afraid to speak up, or thought getting rid of Jesus would help keep the nation safe from Roman brutality.

Our Passover meal was held at a friend of Judas's house in the heart of Jerusalem. It was a two-story home, not counting the roof, and the entire second story was a large banquet room. We were told that many dinners, receptions, and important meetings had been hosted there.

When we gathered, we felt that things were about to change drastically, and we would never be able to go back to the way things had been. I'm certain Jesus felt this way. Looking back, I see clearly that he was talking to us like a man who felt like that evening would be the last conversation he had with those closest to him.

"Friends, I had my hopes but never really thought Simon would come around. I did think some of the other leaders would recognize what we're saying as true. I thought they'd see it as the true heart of our tradition and scriptures. I hate to say it, but now it looks like they are afraid of change and more interested in status and control than truth. I honestly don't understand. I wish I could find the words to help them see that they are clinging to a way of life that will never bring them peace." I remember that as he spoke, he looked around at each of us but seemed to linger on Judas more than the rest of us.

"I think that very soon, maybe even tonight, they will arrest me," again, he looked at Judas, "and, if they do, I don't expect to be returning. If that happens, I will do everything I can to keep them from taking you as

61

well, but obviously we are all in danger. They won't be satisfied to silence just me. They'll want to make sure that each of you will not be a problem as well. We're all in danger." I looked at Judas as Jesus said this, and he was shaking his head in disagreement and had a puzzled look on his face. Jesus continued, "If any of you want to leave, I'll certainly understand. A part of me hopes you do. Maybe you should. Perhaps, if you travel without me and not in a group, you will be able to pass without notice."

"That's not going to happen!" It was Peter, but others were shaking their heads as well. "None of us will leave you, Jesus. Even if some do, even if they all do, it won't be me."

Jesus looked at Peter for several seconds. A chilly wind blew from the windows, and I could hear chickens moving about in the back courtyard, probably making their way to their night time roost. Jesus held his gaze on Peter, like he was assessing him in some way. "I know you mean that, my friend, but you may be expecting too much of yourself. It's going to be hard. Very hard. I'm not totally sure I will see it through. Besides, like I said, if I am arrested, I don't really want you to come with me."

Then Jesus looked around the room at all of us. "What I really want is for you to continue the work. I want you all to realize that you are no longer students or simply followers. You know what you need to know. It's time for you to do it. Live it, do it. Even if you feel unsure, God will guide you. Find a way to follow the Spirit's lead, moment by moment. In every encounter."

I am not sure any of that registered with Peter at all. He continued as if Jesus hadn't spoken. "Jesus, I will not desert you, and arresting you will not be an easy thing to do as long as I am with you. I have a sword. I am not a trained soldier, but I am not afraid, and I am willing to fight." James was still carrying a sword as well, and he was nodding along as Peter spoke. It occurred to me that, if Jesus turned those two loose, we may be safer than I realized. Of course, Jesus had no intention of turning them loose.

"Peter, I am not going to allow you to hurt someone or worse, kill someone, trying to keep me safe. Hear me. Hear me plainly and clearly. I will not allow it. I do not want you to fight, and I do not want you to come with me if they take me. I don't want to be arrested, but, if I am," he hesitated then said quietly, "I will trust God."

The wind stopped, and the chickens had settled. Jesus's attention turned back to Peter, but I think he was really speaking to all of us. "Now listen. Let me give you something. Tonight may turn out to be a very hard night for you. It may be the hardest night of your life, and, when it's over, you may feel like you have failed terribly. But, hear me, the morning will come, and, when the roosters start crowing, remember that I love you and know that you will pass through even your hardest night and fulfill God's purpose for you. Do you hear me?"

"I hear you, but I am not going anywhere, and I do have a sword." Jesus frowned a bit and sighed but let it go. He turned his attention back to the group.

"I have some things that I want to say, and I want you all to remember what I am going to tell you. Perhaps whenever you share a meal you will remember me, recall how I lived, and somehow know that I am with you in a very real way, no matter what." He sighed again but wasn't frowning this time. This time he had something that resembled that look that he got when connecting heart to heart. John was sitting closest to him, and Jesus put his arm around his shoulders and pulled him closer.

"Oh, how I love you all." When Jesus said this, John put his head on Jesus's chest for several seconds. We all did in our imaginations. "I call you friends, but I hope you know it's more. Even more than family. My deepest desire is that you know how much I do love you and that you love each other like that and that you share it with everyone you meet. Surely, we have all learned that God's love knows no bounds. Strangers or people who seem foreign to us are only a part of us that we don't know yet. They are our neighbors. There are no bounds to God's love. You know this, don't you? Look around the room." He paused for a moment, and we did as he instructed. What a group. Fishermen, Zealot, Tax Collector, a drifter, tender hearts, and roughnecks. We all smiled a bit as we got where he was going before he said it. "Who could have pictured this group becoming the band we are." He took a very deep breath, let it out and then he looked around the room like he had told us to, taking each of us in. I couldn't tell if he was trying to see if we understood what he was saying, if he was pondering what he had just said, or if he was trying to memorize everything about us. "I believe with all my heart that if you know how much you mean to me, if you grow in that for one another, you will be experiencing life, true life. Love lasts forever. Knowing that will guide you through anything that can happen."

The meal had been before us this whole time, but no one had touched it until Jesus took some bread, blessed it, broke it, like we'd seen him do so many times, and said, "Here, eat this. Let what I'm saying sink in for a bit. Again, make this a habit when you eat together." Then he actually smiled and said, "Same with wine."

We sat for a minute, thinking about all that we had been through together and how knowing Jesus had changed our lives. I could feel a tear coming down my cheek, and I knew I was not alone. Oh, how I loved him. Oh, how I wished we were in Capernaum eating one of Peter's fish sandwiches. What I wouldn't give for one more journey, one more party, one more moment that made you wonder: How'd he do that?

Judas interrupted our musings. "Jesus, I don't think things are as bad as you think. I still think we can explain what you believe to the leaders in a way that will help them see that we all want the same thing. We all want Israel to be free and great. We all want the world to see that we are God's people and a light for the world. I really believe if we could sit down together, without a crowd around, we could work things out. I think God is going to keep you and all of us safe, and no harm will come to any of us."

Jesus looked at Judas and handed him a piece of the bread that he had broken. "I think you are wrong, my friend. I don't think we want the same thing. I think they are willing to hurt us to protect what they believe is right, but you do what you think you have to do." Judas nodded his head slowly, took a bite of the bread, stood up, went through the door to the outside stairs, and disappeared into the darkness.

We finished our meal and shared some of our favorite memories of our times together. Matthew led us in a couple of songs. Then we walked back to where we were camping, outside the city, at the base of the Mount of Olives.

We had been there about two hours when Judas returned with a company of men that consisted mostly of armed temple guards. There were a few religious leaders. Simon was one of them.

We all stood and Jesus stepped forward. "Hello, friends. Hello, Simon. Why are you here with so many swords and spears?"

Judas looked puzzled for a second, like he hadn't realized that his group would be looked at as an armed guard, but he recovered, walked up to Jesus, hugged him, and kissed his cheek. "I've worked out the meeting I was telling you about." He was going to say something else but things started happening fast and he never got a chance to finish.

Simon came up behind Judas, pushed him out of the way, and commanded the guards to arrest Jesus. Peter and James moved like great cats before the guards took a step. Peter shoved Simon to the ground, causing him to hit the side of his head on a stone. I don't know how they did it all so fast, but both disciples already had their swords out, and they took position by Jesus's side in a way that made me think they had understated their training. But Jesus was quick too. He stepped between them and the guards and shouted, "No! No swords!" Everything went from fast motion to full stop.

Peter and James, all of us, were lost as to what to do next. The guards were as confused as we were. It was like they couldn't figure out who was in charge, Simon or Jesus. Jesus helped Simon to his feet. I guess Jesus was.

"No swords on your part either," he told the guards. "I'm coming with you but only me. Let's go." They started off into the night, forgetting to bind Jesus's hands. Judas ran after them and grabbed Simon's arm.

"Wait, you said he wasn't being arrested. You said you just wanted to talk."

Simon had regained his composure. He looked at Judas, sneered and said, "You stupid, greedy man. Thanks for making this so easy." Then he shouted out to the guards, "Tie that man up! He's a blasphemer and a criminal!" The guards looked chagrined as they did as they were told. It looked like they tied him tighter than they had to, perhaps to make up for forgetting a moment ago.

The look on Judas's face was a mix of disbelief, deep pain, and horror. He stood, with shoulders slumped for a moment as he watched Jesus be led away. Then he turned, shoved his way through our group, and ran away. I heard him begin to sob as he ran past me.

The rest of us stood there in shock. With the exception of Peter and James's brief resistance, we had not said a word or done a thing to help Jesus. Now we were just standing there as a bound Jesus was taken from us.

I began to tremble as I came to the realization that Jesus only had hours to live, and his death was going to be more gruesome than I wanted to think about. I looked at the others as we stood there, and I knew I no longer wanted to be a part of the group. This was not at all what I'd signed up for, not how I thought it would end when I met Jesus at that wedding a few months back. I felt a little bit like Judas. I turned and left them as well.

# Leaving

Jesus was right about our being safe if we weren't with him, even more so if we were alone. I had forgotten what it was like to be a vagabond. You are invisible. People won't even look at you if they can help it.

I stumbled around on the streets of Jerusalem for hours, circling the temple and Pilate's palace in varying patterns, not because I was being sneaky, but because I was unable to do what I really wanted to do. I wanted to walk out of Jerusalem, out of Judea, and out of remembering that the best, most beautiful man I had ever known was about to be executed. I couldn't. I kept circling, occasionally standing close to groups to see if anyone knew anything about what was happening.

"I heard that man from Galilee was arrested."

"I knew they wouldn't let him keep making fools out of them,"

"I heard he was insane, a crazy heretic. I'm glad they got him."

"People like him are dangerous. It doesn't take much to set Rome off, and we all know that when Rome wants to teach a lesson it is a hard one. People get killed."

"They've taken him to Pilate. Doesn't matter what you think of him now. He's done. God, help him."

"They beat him horribly. Whipped him unconscious. His own mother wouldn't recognize him now. They revived him, so they can take him to the execution hill and crucify him. They already had two scheduled. I'm not sure he will still be alive when they hang him up. No way he'll be able to carry the beam up that steep hill."

"Oh God, how can this be happening," my heart cried out. "Let me wake up. Please, let me wake up."

I didn't want to, but, as the morning broke, I found myself looking for a place to stand where I could see the dying men and perhaps still remain unnoticed. When I saw him, the nightmare became real. He was unrecognizable. I told myself that it wasn't really him. It had to be someone else. Surely, they wouldn't have done this to him. Then I saw the scar on his shin that he had shown me when we first met, and my hand instinctively went to the scar on my arm as the awful reality set in.

As terrible as he looked physically, somehow the people standing around watching him and the other two die seemed more revolting. Soldiers were drinking and laughing about how the men on the crosses were struggling to breathe. They were betting on everything: who would die first, which one would beg for mercy, and which one would be the first to curse them. They even gambled for Jesus's robe with his mother looking on.

"To hell with all of you!" It was one of the others being crucified. He spit this out as he painfully lifted himself up to fill his lungs with air. He collapsed downward, pulled himself up again, gasped for air, and then, through grit teeth. "You're sons of bitches, every one of you!" Somehow, he still had enough air to literally spit at the soldiers before collapsing again. They just laughed all the more, and the one that had picked him to be the first to curse held out his hand for payment.

"Jesus, can you help us?" gasped the other man. "Can't you pray," he had to stop and suck in a breath, "and ask God to save us?" When he let himself fall, it was too sudden and he tried to cry out but had no air in his lungs so his face just grotesquely formed the shape of a man crying out, but no noise came out. He strained and pulled himself up again for air and said in a whisper, as he tried to conserve air, "I deserve this, but please take me with you if God comes."

Jesus's jaw muscles showed, even through his bruised and puffy cheeks, as he strained to pull himself up so he could see the man and look into his eyes, "Friend, God is with us," he gasped. Somehow, he held himself up long enough to say, "Death can't separate us from God's love. Be brave, trust me, things are okay, even now."

The slumped man nodded his head, comforted. He seemed to find strength in Jesus's words.

"To hell with you too, Jesus of Nazareth! Your God's not here, he's not anywhere," snarled the cursing man. His anger and hate seemed to be giving him superhuman strength.

"Shut up, Barnabas . . . This is an innocent man . . . Shouldn't be here at all . . . Let him die in peace. Try to die with honor," replied Jesus's new follower between painful gulps.

Along with the soldiers, there was a fairly good size crowd there. Apparently, some of them were there solely to mock Jesus. I didn't see Simon, but others like him were standing at the foot of the cross, asking Jesus if he was going to be teaching today. "Come down and tell us another one of those Samaritan stories!" "I think it's prayer time, Jesus. Come on down and let's go to the temple." And then they would laugh. How could they laugh?

Off to one side but close enough that Jesus could see them when he opened his eyes were the women of our group. Mary was easy to recognize as her robe was the same color and material as Jesus's. Rachel was standing beside her. She looked defiant like she was daring one of the mockers to say a word to her. There were also a couple of men. I am pretty sure one was John, but I couldn't be sure, and I don't know who the other one was as the crowd was blocking my sight.

Suddenly, I heard a voice that I recognized near me. It was Simon's. The reason I hadn't seen him near the cross was because he was actually standing with a couple other leaders just a few feet from me. "I sure hope they don't live very long. It is a holy day, and it's not right to have them hanging there, distracting the people from worship. I'm going to tell the soldiers that they need to break their legs if they aren't dead soon." He walked up to the captain and said something I couldn't hear, but the captain nodded his head in agreement. Then Simon stepped over to Jesus's cross and with a loud voice said, "Jesus, I don't think God is going to get you out of this one. Do you want to say anything to us before you die?"

Everyone was quiet, wanting to hear if Jesus did indeed have anything he wanted to say. Jesus slowly raised his head and looked right at Simon. He held his gaze for a minute in a way that I had seen many times. He actually looked like himself for a moment. He pulled himself up, took in a long breath of air, and slowly said, "I want you to know that I forgive you. You're lost. You have no idea what you are doing."

I couldn't take it anymore. I walked away from that hill, away from the holy city, and headed north. I felt like I was the one that was lost, and I certainly had no idea what I was doing.

# PART 2

# The Path

I'M NOT SURE HOW, maybe it's just where I go when I'm lost, but, after a couple of months of wandering, I found myself back in Corinth. I'd like to say that I handled myself much better this time, but, the truth is, except for avoiding the pagan temples, I was back to my old self, perhaps drinking even more.

Guess I shouldn't have been surprised to wake up in a Roman jail. When I opened my eyes that morning, I had no idea where I was. All I knew was that I was looking at a damp, stone wall, and out of the corner of my left eye I could see where the wall met an equally damp, stone ceiling. I decided that the best thing to do was to stay still and try to do a little remembering. That's exactly what I did, a little remembering, stress on little.

I remembered sitting around a fire with some men behind a cheap inn where some of us wanderers hung around. We were sharing a couple of skins of wine we had gone in together to purchase. I remembered Acco, my tall, muscular friend with long blond hair that he kept tied back. Acco was there. He was about my age and a likable enough guy, and, even though I had decided that I was through liking people, for some reason he had decided he liked me and had stuck with me. Yep, Acco was there. I had drunk my share of the wine way too fast. That was how I drank now. It helped me not think about things that hurt. Actually, it didn't stop the thinking, it just dulled the hurting until the next morning when it hurt even more, so I drank even more.

Try as I might, that's about all I could remember.

I had no idea who the other men had been, where they were, or where I was.

"Hey, you awake?" It was Acco. I followed the sound of his voice and found his rabbit skin boots, so I looked up and saw his leather strap necklace with its silver tree and, eventually, his head. His long hair, that was usually tightly pulled back, sometimes even braided, was loose and tangled. He had apparently had a hard night as well. But, he was smiling. He was almost always smiling.

He was even smiling when he came to my rescue three weeks ago. A couple of thieves had decided they wanted my money pouch, and one of them quietly cut it free from my belt while the other one distracted me by accusing me of stealing a ring. I was oblivious to my pouch leaving my possession because I was pretty sure the chunky fellow in front of me was about to slam one of his ham sized fists into my face in spite of my efforts to convince him that he had the wrong guy.

Acco, whom I had only met a couple of nights before, stepped up like he didn't have a care in the world and asked me if I was sure I didn't want my money anymore. My hand flew to where my pouch used to be and I spun around in time to see the sneaky one put it in his cloak pocket. He left my pouch in his pocket but pulled out a small club.

"I think he wants his money back," said Acco.

"I think you'd be smart to move on," said the thick fellow with ham fists.

Acco kept smiling but something changed in his eyes. They actually looked a little sad. "Give him his money back."

The big fellow threw his huge right fist at Acco's jaw, but Acco's jaw wasn't there anymore. As the fist sailed by, Acco grabbed the man's right shoulder and shoved him hard into the ground. Quicker than a thought, Acco slammed his elbow into the face of the man holding the club, snatched the club, and with a backhand swing knocked the big fellow struggling to get up out cold.

He then held his open hand toward the man whose nose was now gushing blood and the thief quietly reached in his pocket and gave my pouch to Acco, who then handed it to me, and said, "I think we'd be smart to move on." As we walked away, Acco turned back and told the fellow with the bloody nose, "Tell him I'm sorry. I didn't want to." I looked at him to see if he was being sarcastic. There wasn't a bit of sarcasm in his expression. Not a bit.

Acco and I had stayed partners since then. He did occasionally lift my spirits, but I'm not sure what I brought to the relationship I know I never lifted Acco's spirits. I didn't share much of myself, certainly never talked about Jesus and my time following him. Once, when I asked him why he was wandering around Greece, so far from his home in Gaul, he said, "I just feel like I'm looking for something. Something that will give my life meaning."

I looked at him a second with tightened lips, then I looked at the ground as I quietly replied, "There's nothing to find." Again, I'm not sure why he hung with me. Maybe he just felt like I needed him to. I guess I did.

When I decided to completely roll over on my stone bed in the jail, I thought I might throw up as I tried to focus on Acco's face, which was a little out of focus and moving slowly in small circles. "Where are we?"

"Ha! You don't look so good, my friend. We're in jail!" He looked down on me and chuckled. I am not sure if it was because he always seemed to find a way to take things in stride, or if the effects of his night of drinking were still lingering, but he didn't seem to be bothered one little bit that we were locked up in a cold, damp, completely dreary cell.

"How'd we get here?" I was starting to notice that my head hurt a lot more than from a hangover. When I rubbed it, I felt a rather large knot behind my right ear and something sticky that I assumed was some blood that hadn't finished drying. "What happened? Where are the others?"

Acco chuckled again. "We left the others when you got mad at them for asking you too many questions about where you were from and what it was like in Judea. We were taking a little break on the side of the street when the soldiers came by. They told us to stand up and answer some questions. When you couldn't, they thought it was because you were refusing to, so one of them hit you on the side of the head with the butt of his spear, and here we are. You know something? I'm starting to think hanging out with you may not have been my best decision." He made a motion like he was about to lightly hit my head but thought better of it when he remembered my lump.

I looked at him, wondering what it would take to dampen his attitude. I couldn't help but smile a little myself, "I don't know, friend. I'm kinda thinking you're having at least a little fun. Maybe you like jails and think it's funny when your friends get their skulls cracked."

Before he could answer, the door violently swung open. Fortunately, neither of us was close to it, or it would have slammed into us. Two soldiers came in, and I noticed Acco had stopped smiling. He slowly stepped to the side, out of their line of sight and into mine so he could motion some kind of a message to me. He looked very concerned, and, when he acted like he was getting hit in the head, I got that he was telling me that one of them was the fellow I could thank for the bloody lump.

"Well good morning, street scum. Who wants a nice big breakfast? Fruit? Bread? A little sip of wine to clear your head?" He paused for a second, looked at me, and lunged, raising his spear as if to strike me. "Maybe another thump to go with last night's?"

I flinched, and he laughed.

The one talking was at least a head shorter than Acco and thinner by a lot. But his uniform fit him perfectly, and it had every extra button or badge soldiers were allowed to wear. There was an eagle brand on his right shoulder that I assumed was part of some kind of fraternity. "I'm thinking we could just skip breakfast and just go straight to the post for our forty lashes. What do you think, Cornelius?" The short, loud man asked his companion.

"Come on, Marcus," answered the soldier called Cornelius. "They're just drunks. They aren't getting whipped for sleeping on the street."

"We don't know that they're just drunks. We have no idea what they did before we saw them or what they would do if we let them go. Street scum. That one there," he nodded toward me, "had a little money. I wonder how he got it?"

He then looked at Acco, "You, you're not Greek. Where are you from? What's your name."

"I am Acco, a Celt from a place you call Gaul."

"Gaul? Acco? There was a king named Acco who fought against Rome from Gaul. You aren't him are you?"

Acco smiled, "I think you know he's been dead for some time. I was named for him."

"You see, Cornelius? We have an insurgent right here in our jail. A rebel from Gaul. You, where are you from?" he asked me.

I looked at the floor and answered, "I'm from Judea, the land of Israel."

"Judea? Not exactly known for its loyalty to Caesar either. I should know, I was on assignment there till a few weeks ago. In Jerusalem, a part of Pilate's guard." I guess I flinched again when I heard that because something made him continue, "Pilate knows how to handle insurgents. You ever hear of Jesus from Nazareth?" I didn't say anything, but he sensed that he was hitting a sore spot and pressed further. "I asked you a question, Jew. Have you heard of Jesus from Nazareth?"

"Yes. I actually met him."

"Ha! Well, you won't be meeting him anymore, will you? Like I said, Pilate knows how to deal with rebels. Hey, wait a minute. You know what? You and Jesus have something in common that may interest you. You both were hit by the butt end of my spear." He laughed like realizing that had made his day.

"Come on, Marcus." It was the one called Cornelius. "These guys are harmless. You're such an ass." He looked at his fellow soldier and shook his head. The look on his face showed that he truly found Marcus trying, to say the least. "I don't know why you have to be like that, but I'm getting tired of it."

"Shut up, Cornelius! Just because you are about to be promoted and reassigned doesn't mean you can start giving me orders." I hadn't heard an order, just an observation that I happened to agree with, but I didn't share my thoughts. "If you won't believe my stories about how horrible it is to serve in that land, you can ask street scum here. You should be the one interrogating him. You might learn something. I bet he could give you some insight as to what you're in for." Then he looked back at me, "He's headed to your homeland, Jew. Getting a big promotion. Tell him how much a Roman officer will like it there, how everybody loves Rome and respects its officers. Tell him about the Zealots." He continued, "I'll tell you what. We can find out about these pieces of rebel scum right now. I've got a question for you both, and you better answer quickly and answer correctly. Is Caesar lord, your lord? Does the emperor have your allegiance?"

He looked at Acco. Acco looked back and with that perpetual smile on his face answered, "I can't imagine anyone or anything more powerful. He's my lord, or I don't have one." Marcus smiled and nodded, apparently not catching that my friend hadn't actually answered his question.

"You," he stepped closer to me. "Repeat after me, and mean it. Caesar is my lord. I owe him my all."

I shrugged and looked back at him, "Sure, Caesar is my lord. I owe him my all."

"To the gods!" He shouted. You're both pitiful! You aren't even decent rebels. Street scum! Another night in jail for you then you can go and drink your sorry asses to death." He turned and left. Cornelius looked at us a second and seemed to be considering saying something, perhaps an apology for his colleague's behavior, perhaps asserting his authority and letting us go, but he didn't do any of that. He walked out, slowly shutting and locking the door behind him.

They didn't leave any breakfast, and Acco and I both knew we'd have the same for dinner. I lay back down and turned back toward the wall. As I went back to sleep or maybe passed back out, I don't know which, I could feel my head pounding, but its pain was nothing compared to the heavy weight on my heart.

Late that night, probably to keep from thinking about how hungry we were as much as anything, Acco and I started talking about our lives, and, for the first time since the crucifixion, I shared about my time with Jesus. After I had talked for about a half hour Acco said, "He was, I can't really think of the word for it."

"The word I use is 'beautiful.' He was beautiful."

"Yes, beautiful and more. It sounds like he made others beautiful too. Especially those that thought they were something else."

"You've got it. If everyone else cast you off, you had a friend in Jesus."

"Even street scum like you?"

I smiled. "Sure felt like it. Not sure what he'd think if he were alive and saw me now."

We were quiet for a bit, and I truly pondered what Jesus would think if he saw me there in the jail cell, unable to remember much of the last several days.

Acco broke the silence, "Friend, what are you going to do when we get out tomorrow?"

"You heard the man. Drink my sorry ass to death."

"Ha! I have a better plan. Something I've been thinking about for a month or so now. Come with me on a journey. An adventure. A pilgrimage."

"I'm on a journey now. Far from home, getting further."

"I'm serious. Come with me to my hometown, let me say hello to my family, I'll introduce you, then let's walk the sacred path out of Gaul, through Spain, to the end of the world."

"What in the world are you talking about? What sacred path through Spain to the end of the world?"

"It's a sacred path that starts near my hometown in Gaul and goes over mountains, through forests, and through many holy spots, places that seem closer to heaven than earth. It ends where the earth ends, as far west as you can go. Wise ones, men and women with strong spirits, travel it. They lead others to do the same or help them prepare. They say it's a path that calls those who are lost and hope to find themselves. They say walking can bring wisdom, enlightenment."

I softly said, "Well, if anyone's lost . . ."

"Think about it. I'm told those who walk it find peace. They say it changes you. Changes you into someone who can help others find peace. I'm tired of living like this. I'm tired of wandering, doing nothing. There has to be more to life than waking up in jail and being called names by some puffed up Roman bully. They say the people along the way expect travelers and are very hospitable. If nothing else, we can tell people we have seen where land ends in the west. Come with me. Let's do it."

I told him I'd think about it, and drifted off, cold, hungry, hurting, feeling as lost as I ever had, thinking about it.

When the morning came it was Cornelius that let us out. As I walked past him on my way through the door, he handed me the money that I had been carrying when they arrested us. It actually wasn't the same money, it was different coins but it was the same amount. I figure Marcus had the original coins and the ones Cornelius handed me came from his own purse.

I stopped for a moment, "I wish you well on your new appointment. My people just want peace and to be treated fairly. It's not as bad as Marcus makes it."

"I don't listen to Marcus. Take care of yourself." He paused, then added, "I don't think you're street scum."

Before I could think to stop myself I said, "Jesus, the other one he hit with his spear, would say there's no such thing as street scum."

Cornelius looked in my eyes and said, "I think I believe that myself. I would have liked to have met this Jesus. Of course, he probably didn't care much for Roman soldiers."

A lump was suddenly in my throat but I choked out, "Actually he did. Roman soldiers, everybody."

We walked outside, and Acco took a deep breath, "Oh my, the air tastes better out here." He looked up at the sun, pointed to his left and said, "North. I'm off. North for a while then west, west, west; till I run out of land." He took another deep breath and looked at me, "You coming?"

The moment felt very familiar. "Yes, yes I am."

# Preparation

I LEARNED THERE ACTUALLY was something that could dampen Acco's sunny attitude: ocean water. It was his plan to walk home, avoiding water, and adding weeks to his journey. He hated to be at sea. He couldn't stand to be out of sight of land because it turns out, he couldn't swim, even a little bit. He was truly afraid of deep water. It took me a couple of days, but, after a lot of cajoling, I convinced him that, if we wanted to make it to his home by winter, we needed to get on a boat a couple of times. Before he could change his mind, I bought us both passage on the next ship to Rome.

On that leg of the journey, I made friends with the captain, I sold him on my carpentry skills, and he gave me a job making various kinds of repairs. That let me earn a little money for the second part of our journey. Once we were in Rome, it only took us a couple days to find a ship headed for Spain.

Miraculously, we only had stormy weather one time while we were at sea, but that one time was plenty rough. The waves were higher than the ship's masts, and more than once I felt sure they would swallow us. Things got so bad that the captain threw a good bit of the cargo over to make us lighter and higher in the water. I guess it worked because we didn't get swamped and sink, but we were so light it felt like we were a pine cone that the giant waves were using in a game of catch. Acco was terrified, almost crying. I didn't show it like he did, but I was right there with him. I'm pretty sure the captain and other sailors were shaken as well. All of us were half laughing, half weeping from joy, and saying "thank yous" to our various gods and lucky charms when we could see a little blue in the sky.

After the storm passed and we had survived, it looked to me like Acco had calmed down a little. I thought it would be kinda funny to tell him the story of Jonah and the great fish that swallowed him. I added that he could have been our Jonah, and we probably should have thrown him in the water to stop the storm earlier. That was a mistake, a cruel mistake. He told me that he probably was our Jonah, and he should never have set foot on a ship. I don't think he slept more than twenty minutes at a time until we made landfall. I've never seen a person who was happier than Acco was when we walked down that gang plank and began our hike north toward Gaul.

While he was completely useless on water, Acco more than made up for it on land. He was an expert hunter and gatherer. He provided rabbits and pheasants almost daily. Plus, he found all kinds of plants, roots, and berries to eat in the forest. He got more information out of reading trees, rocks, earth, and sky than the most diligent scribes get out of reading scrolls. He could find food, water, and the best trails seemingly without effort. We were walking in a wilderness that would have bewildered me if I had been alone, but for weeks I never once was thirsty, hungry, or felt like we were lost.

He did all this with a certain reverence. He never broke a limb on a bush unless he needed to so we could pass. He thanked the rabbits we had for dinner for giving their lives so we could continue. He walked so quietly, that I felt like I was stomping as I followed him along the paths that I didn't see until we were on them.

When I asked him about his skill in the wilderness, he told me that his people had a relationship with creation, and it was second nature for him to make his way in the forest. He said that he had noticed that many cultures don't think of themselves as a part of nature. They seemed to either ignore it whenever they could or they sought to conquer it. "My people live with creation, not in competition. We don't seek to subdue it. We are a part of it. It's our source of life. You'll see when we get to my village. Even the houses are different from the ones you're used to. They are round, like the sun and moon, not boxes. We're thankful for what the earth gives us. We don't take more than we need. You'll see. It's very different from Rome and Corinth. It'll be good to get home."

"I've noticed that you talk like dirt, trees, and animals can hear you. Like they can understand you."

"They can, and they can talk back. The land will tell you what it needs, animals will feel respect and take care of you, trees will tell you which way to go if you know their language. The earth provides."

"Wait, you really and truly talk to trees?"

His grin was ear to ear, "Yes, I do, but not like you think. I know their language. You have to learn their language then you know they are talking all the time."

I couldn't tell how much he was teasing me or how serious he was. I had the feeling that he was actually more serious than teasing. "Great. I'm in the middle of Gaul's wilderness with a man that talks to trees."

He laughed. "Everything in creation talks. Trees, animals, water, stones. Not in words but they speak."

"Everything?"

"Yes. Everything."

"The sea?"

"Of course the sea talks."

"Oh really? What does the sea say?"

"Easy. Keep the hell off me." I shook my head and threw a stick at my friend's feet.

In that laugh with a friend, I realized that, in the middle of a talking wilderness, on a journey with a purpose, my heart was starting to heal. Perhaps it was because Jerusalem was so far away and felt like a different world, or maybe walking in the woods was washing away hurt and disappointment, or maybe, having a friend is simply good for the soul. Whatever the reason, I was getting my balance and starting to feel alive.

It didn't hurt so much to talk about Jesus with Acco. In fact, I found that I wanted to share my stories and memories more and more. And Acco wanted to hear them. Often, he would have an insight as to where Jesus was coming from that I hadn't seen until Acco put his spin on it. When I told him about the great commandments, to love God and our neighbors as ourselves, his response was, "Of course, our neighbors are a part of us. We love them as they are a part of us. We are all connected, all a part of the same creation. I get it."

Almost every night he would ask me to tell him something else Jesus had done or said. "Tell me another Jesus story," he would say. "When you talk about him it makes me think he was a Celt. Only a Celt would see that much spirit in the sky and stones."

If Acco was representative, I could see why he said that. Acco would often look at the clouds in a way that reminded me of Jesus looking at the sky over the Sea of Galilee. Acco also had a habit of holding a stone as he sat and meditated in the evenings. I once asked him why he did that. He just shrugged and said he enjoyed thinking about what all the stone had seen, he liked feeling its spirit in his hands. I remembered Jesus talking about stones that praise God.

He liked the story about the big dinner.

"Once we were on one of our trips, we were far from any town. Somehow a bunch of people had found out where we were, and, since a prayer or blessing from Jesus seemed to help sick folks more than the doctors could, they brought their sick friends and relatives in droves. It was a wonderful day, so wonderful everyone lost track of time.

"When Andrew noticed that the sun would be setting in a couple of hours, he told Jesus he needed to send the folks away. They wouldn't get to their towns till after dark as it was. Jesus said, 'Nope, I think I'm going to ask them to stay. Let's have a banquet.'

"We were all astounded. 'Jesus,' Andrew said, 'I'm not sure we have enough for us, let alone all these people. Even if there was a town nearby where we could buy some food, we don't have near enough money to feed this many people.' Well, there was this little boy, not more than ten years old, who had been hanging around Jesus all day. He was standing there and had heard all this. He tugged on Jesus and offered his five loaves and two fish, just enough for his own lunch. Jesus looked at us like, see? Then he said, 'Get everyone seated and tell them we're about to eat.'

"Peter told the rest what was going on and enlisted our help in getting everyone situated. Frankly, we were all dumbfounded. Eat? Banquet? What? But we did as we were told. 'Folks, take a seat,' we said, 'Sit with your family, sit with your friends, or sit with people you want to get to know. Just sit in a small enough group that there can be some fellowship. We're about to start the banquet.' Now everyone was dumbfounded. 'Banquet?' they said. 'Where's the food coming from?' they said. We heard it over and over, but, like us, they went along.

"Jesus took the boy's lunch, held it for a moment, gave thanks, then blessed it, broke it into pieces, and gave each of us a little bit and said, 'Go feed them. They're hungry.' Man, I can't tell you how silly we felt walking up to a bunch of people who were waiting to be served, and all we had was a little piece of bread and a little chunk of fish—"

"I love it," Acco interrupted me, like he did pretty much every time I told the story and I got to this part. "A boy offered his little meal, Jesus took it, blessed it, and everyone ate! How in the world?"

"Well, like I've told you, when I got to my group, I saw some folks reach in their packs and pull out food that we didn't know they had. Of course, folks aren't going to go that far into nowhere without packing something. Anyway, it was two things. On the one hand, folks started sharing food that they had been holding back, and, on the other hand, I just never ran out. I'd give people fish and bread, and I just kept having fish and bread to give. It was crazy. Crazier still, when we were through, everyone was full, felt like it had been a banquet indeed, and we had more than enough left over to last us the rest of the journey.

"And, that's a day in the life with Jesus. Somehow there's enough, somehow you get where you're supposed to be when you are supposed to be there, and interwoven in all of it is generosity, trust, and thanksgiving."

"I love that story. Everything about it." he said.

I smiled at my friend and said, "I know you do."

Acco smiled back, then his face grew serious, "Have you noticed that you often talk about Jesus as if he is still alive?"

I didn't answer. I didn't know what to say. I just felt a familiar sting in my heart and said nothing.

It's a good thing I talked Acco into taking those two sea-legs on our journey because when we reached his village in its beautiful valley, winter was right behind us.

The greeting Acco got when we arrived was reminiscent of my own when I returned to the farm except this time a whole town was rejoicing. Of course, he had left on better terms. Everywhere we turned another cousin was coming up to hug him and ask about his adventures.

One cousin, an older, taller, thicker version of Acco, grabbed him, threw him to the ground, and attempted to pin him. Acco somehow twisted away, sprang to his feet, lifted his arms in the air, and shouted, "Ha! My old cousin still thinks he can bully me! I figured out how to get out of that one while I was away!"

The older man got up, shaking with laughter. "Well, it took you long enough!" Then he lunged at Acco and said, "Now, I'll show you the counter to the counter!" He didn't though. They just hugged and slapped each other on the back.

The older cousin's wife was tall, athletic looking, and had wavy red hair that covered her shoulders and fell halfway down her back. When she walked up to give her welcome home hug, she called out Acco's name and congratulated him for besting her husband. She seemed very glad to see Acco and hugged him tightly, but I noticed a little hesitancy on Acco's part. It was quick, but it was there. His hug was lighter and broke off sooner than most of the others. Her name was Sucaria.

The entire village was filled with gracious people. They welcomed me like I was a new member of the family. I got almost as many back slaps, hugs, and offers of drinks as Acco. The big cousin, Sucaria's husband, even said he was going to see if I could escape his special pin move. Thankfully, he was just teasing me.

All this welcoming and hugging, with a lot of food, wine, music and dancing thrown in, lasted a few days, but we eventually settled into what Acco called our winter's work. This work was essentially to prepare our hearts for the journey we would take when spring arrived.

There were several people in the village that had walked the path to the end of the earth, and they all had some advice and directions that would come in handy. The one that was primarily charged with getting us ready though was the village's acknowledged wise one: an elderly woman that everyone called "Mother." I found it a little strange to be tutored by a woman, but Acco acted like it was the most natural thing in the world.

I don't think Mother had ever been married, and she had no children that I ever met, but she was Mother just the same. When she was a young woman, she had walked the path alone. Over the years she had walked it several more times as a guide and mentor for others. Now she was too old to make the journey, but she still helped prepare people like Acco and me who were about to make their own journey. In fact, I was told that it wasn't unusual for people to come from other villages to be mentored by her for their walk to the sea.

One mild winter evening, just after the sun had set, but before it was truly dark, Mother, Acco, and I sat together around her fire pit as she lit the night's fire. As the flame grew, she told us, like she had many times, that we were about to walk a path like no other. She said the path itself had a spirit and would always provide what we needed. "Walking this path will change your life if you trust it and open yourself to its gifts." That seemed like a pretty big thing to say about a trail, but it did stir something in me. I was starting to wonder if trees, paths, birds, and rocks did indeed have a little magic in them. I wondered if my life would take a turn as I walked. I wondered what that turn would look like.

Mother was one of the tiniest people I have ever seen. One could say that she was no bigger than a bird. Her long nose, the raven tattoo on her right forearm, and feathers from all kinds of birds tied in her hair certainly gave her a bird-like look.

She took Acco's relationship with creation to a whole new level. Often, she would tell me about someone with whom she had been sorting something out, and I would realize that she wasn't talking about having a conversation with another human, she was talking about a deer, a huge stone, or an ancient tree. And, like Acco, she was deeply interested in Jesus and soaked up everything I could tell her about him. Just as Acco had, she quickly jumped on the part about Jesus saying that we are to love others as ourselves. She too said that he didn't mean to love like you love yourself, but to love your neighbor because they were a part of you. Mother would nod her head when she spoke of this and always closed saying, "It's all one. We are one, creation is one, God is the One."

Our preparation was almost daily and consisted mostly of her telling us again and again that we were embarking on a sacred journey, not just an adventure. A lot of time was spent trying to help me learn to read what was going on around me in the wilderness. She said it mostly came down to paying attention, noticing details, and pondering them. I would never get on her or Acco's level, but I did begin to see things with new eyes.

As we sat around fires waiting for snow to melt, took long walks on warmer days, and ate various stews with her most nights; she pushed us to discern what it was that was calling us to go on this pilgrimage to the end of the world. She told us to try and figure out what we were seeking in our truest hearts. One night Acco was with his parents, and it was just Mother and me. She told me that she was cold and asked me to put some more wood on the fire. As the flames grew and we both appreciated the heat, she said, "Ask yourself why. Really ask yourself why you feel called to make this journey, and keep asking until you have an honest answer to that question."

"I'm not sure I'm really called," I replied. "I may be going simply because I don't know what else to do. Maybe I just want to see the end of the earth. Hang out with Acco." I looked into the fire for a long moment. "Not sure I'm called at all. Not sure there's anything that calls."

"You're called. All those things are whispers. You're called. Ask yourself why." She took a sip of her hot mead and stared at me like she knew the answer but wasn't going to tell me. Her gaze made me uncomfortable so I stared into my beer. I didn't know the answer, and wondered if I ever would.

That's how we spent the winter. Looking into our hearts, learning to pay attention.

It was decided that our day of departure would be spring's equinox. When that was about a week away, Mother summoned us to her tiny house one morning in order to give us our final instructions. When we got there, Acco called inside to let her know we had arrived and we took our seats around her outdoor fire pit that was still warm from the previous night. It was surrounded by stones that Mother had collected and pottery she had formed. Out of some of the pots, herbs were growing, others held smaller rocks, and one was filled with black ink. There was a long sharp needle beside it.

Mother came out after a few minutes, sat down, and without any small talk to warm up, began, "Before you go, find a stone to carry with you. Don't just walk away this morning and pick up the first one you see. Wait till you find the one that is calling you. Put it in your pack and feel its weight as you travel. When you get to the highest hill of your journey, take your stone from your pack and place it at the foot of the ancient tree that will be there. Before you release it, give it whatever it is that keeps you from becoming your true self. You will know where to put it when you see it. There will be a large pile of rocks there already because for a long time people have been sensing that this is a sacred place, and they have been placing stones there as an offering to their gods. That's not what you are doing. I am not talking about a superstition. I am talking about you releasing what hinders you from becoming you.

"I want you to remember that each of us is a part of the Creator, and the highest task we have is becoming our true self—letting go of whatever it is that keeps us from doing that."

I thought I needed a little more guidance on what would keep me from becoming my true self, but all she would give me was, "You'll need to find that answer for yourself. It could be something like a regret that is taking up too much space in your heart. Some people find that selfishness has over-taken them. Others vanity. For some it's fear or anxiety." She looked directly at me and added, "Others, an unwillingness to do the work they know they need to do to become their true selves. You'll know when you get there."

She also told us to ask someone who had died to travel with us as a guide and companion. That sounded a little hokey to me, but I went along and respectfully asked my father to come along. Acco said, "I am asking your friend, Jesus, to be my guide and show me the way."

I said, "Well, if anyone can, he can."

The last thing on Mother's morning agenda had to do with the ink and needle. Mother told us that she wanted to give us a tattoo of her choosing to remind us of our purpose. I told her that I would have to pass on that one, but Acco got his and since I couldn't read their language I had to ask him what it said.

"To find and be truly you," he said.

# The Journey West

THE EQUINOX WAS COMING and we were packed and ready to go. The only problem was that a couple of days before we were scheduled to start our journey a cold front hit, and, along with colder temperatures, it brought rain, a bunch of rain. It was freezing, and rain was coming down like buckets. I had spent a good portion of my life outside, and I could brave the cold and endure the rain, but I never could stand cold and wet together.

I knew that there was no way we would completely avoid foul weather during a two or three month walk out of Gaul and across Spain, but I was more than willing to wait for a more favorable send off. Acco, however, was determined to start on the equinox and was insistent that we leave as planned. He was convinced that the cold and wet were part of the process, and our task was to endure it if we wanted to receive the full benefit of our quest.

"It's a gift that we start with a trial. It's a sign that we're on the right path, and something wonderful awaits us." His reasoning seemed a little shaky to me. In fact, I felt like I could have made the argument that it was a sign that we were supposed to wait, but I consented. A little before dawn on the day of the spring equinox we were off. In spite of the miserable weather Acco's family, Mother, and half the village were bundled up and lined along the path out of town to send us on our way.

"Good journey!"

"Remember us when you get there!"

"We'll be praying for a safe journey!"

We heard them calling until their voices slowly mixed in with the rain drops hitting the leaves. Finally, they completely faded, and all we heard was the wind and rain pummeling the forest. We were on our way west, to the end of the earth. I still wasn't completely sure why I was making this trip, but, even in the cold and the wet, I somehow felt like I was right where I was supposed to be. I felt alive, joyful even. I would not have imagined that I would ever feel like that again after experiencing that horrible morning in Jerusalem.

If the cold and rain were a gift to enrich our journey, four days later we received another one. I got sick, really sick. My throat was on fire, I was so congested I could barely breathe, and I developed a cough so bad that a couple of times I coughed uncontrollably until I passed out. It took a huge amount of effort to make myself swallow, and breathing was such a chore that often I had to concentrate on one breath at a time. I must have looked and sounded as bad as I felt because Acco said he was going to make a stretcher and try to drag me back to his village where I could be cared for. I told him that was not possible. He couldn't drag me that far, and I simply couldn't make the trip even if he could. I would just need to rest, stay hydrated, and try to force myself to take nourishment. So, he put together a little shelter, built a fire, and tried to keep me supplied with rabbit stew and herbal tea.

At first I seemed to be descending. I had no energy at all, and I slept all through the day, except for when Acco would wake me for food and drink. This lasted for two complete days. During those times of sleep, I had some of the most realistic dreams I have ever experienced.

I dreamed that I made it back to the farm after my travels, my brother rejoiced in my return just as my father had. In the dream he had gotten married and introduced me to his wife and my two nieces. It was so wonderful and felt so good that I was laughing and crying at the same time. Apparently I was doing so in real life as well because Acco said that heard me making noise as I slept, but he couldn't tell if it was a happy noise or sad.

In another one I was walking with Jesus along the Sea of Galilee, and he was asking me where I got the crazy idea that he was dead. I told him all about the last days in Jerusalem, how tragic his death had been, how sad and brokenhearted he looked, and how distressed I had been since then. I said that I had no words to express how happy I was that he was safe. This dream ended with him looking over my shoulder, I think at his mother, and asking her if she had ever heard of such a funny thing, then they both laughed. It was so beautiful to hear them laughing like that again that I started laughing as well. My laughter hurt my throat and woke me. Oh, how I wished those dreams were as real as they felt.

I did finally start to feel better. After those two days of sleep, I told Acco I was ready to start walking again, but he said that we should give me another day or two because we were close to the first of our mountain climbs. That night, I felt like I had enough strength to chat a bit, so I asked Acco something I had been wondering since we'd met. "Acco, why'd you ever leave your village? You love it there, they love you, it fits you way better than the streets of Corinth. I've always felt like it was more than you getting a little wanderlust."

He looked at me from the other side of our fire for several seconds before speaking. "I'm going to tell you the truth," his hands were balled into fists and he bit his lower lip, "something I've never said out loud. Sucaria. It kills me to be around her," as I looked at the fire reflecting in his blue eyes, they looked moist. "We were best friends growing up. She was a better hunter than me, could run almost as fast as me, laughed at the same things as me.

"I love her. She loves my cousin.

"I thought wandering around the Roman world would make me forget or something. Now I'm hoping part of what this walk does is help me let go." I looked at him, thinking he'd want to say more. "I'm not going to say anything else about this. Ever." And, he didn't.

Four days later, when we had finally finished our day-long ascent, I thanked him profusely for having the wisdom to make me rest those extra two days. I was absolutely exhausted.

He laughed and said, "Oh don't worry, they tell me that there is more to come. In fact, the highest point is not for a few weeks.

"Do you still have your stone? Remember we are supposed to leave it there, on the highest mountain, letting go of whatever keeps us from being our true selves."

I told him that I had followed Mother's instructions and found a stone that I felt like had called me and it was in my pack. I also told him that if he kept talking about mountains, I was going to hit him with it. Like I said, I was exhausted. We had gone up for hours and hours, miles upon miles, and I was done. I ate a little bread and some dried meat that we still had from the village, lay down, and was asleep before the night's second star came out.

It's hard to describe the next few weeks. We walked through pastures, through forests, up hills, down hills, along miles of straight, rocky roads; sometimes accepting the hospitality offered along the way, often sleeping outside. We walked and walked, always west. On clear days it was sun on our backs in the morning, and in our face as the day came to an end. On rainy days it was wet and chill, all over, all day. Always we anticipated what it would be like to be finished, and we talked about what being at the end of the earth would feel like. Walking was our life. It was what we did; rise early, walk all day, eat together, tell some stories, laugh a lot, complain a bit about our pains, sleep, and do it all again. Day after day after day. It was hard. It was a little scary. It was wonderful. I felt centered, hopeful. I found myself occasionally looking at the sky, and I realized that I now smiled when I remembered Jesus instead of hurting.

And, while I didn't have the words for it then, I am not sure I was even totally aware of the feeling, somewhere in my heart I knew this walk was a walk into a new chapter, a changed life. I sure see that now.

One day as we were walking through some woods that we had been in most of the day and didn't seem to have an end, Acco said, "We are getting close to a town. Perhaps tonight we will make some new friends and have something besides camp cooking for supper."

"Acco, we are in the middle of the woods. There's barely a path! What makes you think we are getting close to a town?"

"The woods told me. You know I can speak their language. Mother tried to teach you, but I guess you weren't a very good student." I thought I noticed a little smile.

Lo and behold, a little less than a half mile later we came up on the outskirts of a small town and were greeted by the barking of several large, shaggy dogs with huge heads. They lived on the streets and served as sentinels. We did, indeed, make some new friends.

When we passed an older couple who were working in their garden, they invited us for the evening meal and to spend the night in their house. They said they often offered hospitality to pilgrims on the walk. They were delightful. It was a wonderful meal of perfectly grilled beef, tomatoes, spinach, delicious bread, and good wine.

When I told them I was from Judea they surprised me and said that another traveler from my home country had come by a few months ago. They said he was a big man and had tried to tell them about our religion. They were a little sketchy on what his message had been, but said it had something to do with a man that had died but came back to life. They asked if all Jews believed this way. I told them that I had never heard such a thing, and he may have been a little off in the head. They laughed and said that is what they had thought too.

They asked us if we wanted to stay with them for a few more days so we could rest up before continuing. It was tempting, but we thanked them and declined. They seemed genuinely sorry and gave us enough food to last for a week. The next morning, as was our practice, Acco and I rose before dawn and got back on the path.

After we had walked for an hour or so, I asked Acco how he had known we were so close to a town.

"I told you. The woods told me. We Celts have the ability to hear the woods talk and understand. Since you aren't able, it must be a magic that only we possess." This time I definitely saw the smile.

"Oh, come on, tell me!" his smile turned to a grin, and his shoulders shook a little from a chuckle, "I don't believe you. You better come up with a better answer than you're magic."

"No, I'm actually quite magical. I'd love to tell you how we do it, but there is no way you could understand. Magic."

"You're full of dung! Tell me how you knew!"

Now he laughed out loud and said, "Okay, since you used the magic word, perhaps you are able to comprehend. I'll give you this one lesson in magic. You remember all those dogs that barked at us when we were coming into town? Actually, they were the ones that magically told me." He paused and laughed at his own joke that I still didn't get. "When we were getting close to town, I started seeing more dog turds, and that told me a town was close." Then he couldn't help himself, "So you see, I am not only magic, I know shit."

I just shook my head, trying not to let him know that I was actually impressed by his gift of observation. Not so much his sense of humor. That night's story about Jesus was the one about the woman that reminded us that since even dogs get crumbs from the table a mother who loves her daughter is worth an empathetic ear.

As we continued our journey, it was curious to me that there always seemed to be a path almost always headed due west except when rivers or other geological obstacles caused a detour. Sometimes the path was wide and obvious, a well-traveled road. Sometimes it was more narrow and overgrown. Sometimes it was a gully with large stones that made it hard to walk without twisting an ankle. Sometimes it was through a pasture with sloping hills. All the time, we could see the path, and we never felt like we had lost it.

Acco said he could feel the difference in his heart when we took a detour to hunt or look for a market. "Don't you feel it?" he asked one day. "I feel lighter and more assured that we will be okay when we're on the path. I feel like nothing can happen that we can't deal with." I never felt a connection like that, but I was convinced that our journey was sacred, and I did feel a certain peace when we were on the path, making our way west.

It was obvious Acco and I weren't the only ones who felt like the path was holy because we often passed a stack of rocks that had been used as an altar or some kind of sacred carving on one of the chestnut trees.

One night we camped with a fellow pilgrim who was making his way back to his home a little north of Acco's village. He and Acco had never met, but they talked about places in the area that both were familiar with, and our guest had heard of Mother. He shared some information about villages ahead and various landmarks. He didn't say much about his inner experience, only that he was glad that he had made the journey, and that he felt like he had been changed. "I'm not sure how to describe it," he said. "I just know that I'm more certain about who I am, and clearer about how I want to live." Then he just smiled and said, "Maybe you'll see for yourself." Then he turned to his side and fell fast asleep.

A couple of weeks later we were climbing again. It wasn't as steep as when we started, but it was steady, and it was definitely a climb. Late one morning we came to a large pile of stones almost eight feet high. Some of the stones had symbols scratched on them, others had a couple of letters painted on the sides that probably were shorthand for a message the travelers that had left them wanted to offer.

"This has got to be the place," said Acco. "Look around, there are no hills higher than this one. This is where we leave our stones and walk away free of the pain and hindrances that keep us from the gift of the path."

With that he walked to the other side of the pile, knelt, shed his pack, and pulled out his stone. I think his facing the path we had been traveling was intentional. Everything he did seemed to hold a special meaning. It was obvious that he had given a lot of thought as to what he intended to do here. I wondered if Sucaria was a part of what his stone held.

He held it in both hands for a minute or so, and then he extended his arms like he was offering it to the pile. After a few seconds of holding this posture he gently placed his stone on the pile, stood, and started walking west on the new path.

As he walked away, I realized that I had been watching him and hadn't even taken my stone out of my pack. I thought about doing exactly what Acco had done, but then realized that, if this was going to be something that meant anything to me, I needed it to be authentic, not simply mimicking my friend.

I took my stone out of my pack. It was a river rock. I had carried it over two hundred miles, and it had started feeling like it held a part of me. I noticed its cool smoothness in my left hand as I walked up to the pile that had taken several years to accumulate and reverently placed my right hand on the holy stack. I thought about all the pain, prayers, and hopes that each of those stones represented, and it occurred to me that a prayer for my fellow travelers that had been here before me would be appropriate. Then I realized that I hadn't even thought about praying since that last meal with Jesus and the others, and I wasn't sure what to say.

Jesus had told us that if we were breathing we were praying, and, in that moment, I hoped that was true. I stumbled for a moment, trying to think of some decent prayer. Then it came to me, simply praying like Jesus had taught me was probably enough, so I slowly whispered, "Our Father in

Heaven, your will be done. Today, give us our daily bread. Forgive us, as we forgive. Lead us in your way, and deliver us from evil."

When I prayed the part about forgiving, I thought about Simon and the last time I had seen him. Jesus had forgiven him, but I wasn't sure I could. I silently added, "Help me with that if you can."

After that I finally focused my attention on my stone. I looked at its now familiar streaks, felt its smoothness and weight in my hand one last time, and wished I had given more thought as to what I wanted to leave there.

I had a lot of choices. The guilt I felt for what I had done to my father and brother, the heavy grief I carried for Jesus, and the anger, perhaps hate, I felt for Simon and those who had killed Jesus were certainly front runners. I gazed at my stone and thought about how it didn't have anything on it. I hadn't scratched any symbols or painted any messages, there was only a thin crack along one side.

Then I knew if the point was to become my true self, I couldn't leave any of the things I was considering because they were a part of who I was. I had hurt my family, I was grieving, and I did have hard feelings for Simon and the others. That was part of who I was. If the point was to be truly me, that was truly me. But I also realized that wasn't all of me. I had a fine traveling companion, I was hopeful, and I did feel called to be on this path. That felt like enough for that day. Anything else would have just been playing and pretending. So, I placed my stone on the pile, thanked it for traveling with me for so long, wished it well on its next path, and hurried to catch up with my friend.

# The End of the Earth

WE GOT THERE. IT felt like it took a lifetime, not because it took so long, but because it felt like walking to the end of the earth was our life. It was what we did. The journey had become such a part of who we were it was surreal to be there, where land ended and only the ocean lay to the west. We couldn't walk any further west if we wanted to.

It was sensory overload. The ocean's smell, the cloudless blue sky meeting the darker blue water, waves crashing into the rocks below us, the feel of the sun in our faces—and the wind. It was breathtaking, literally, breathtaking due to the powerful wind coming off the churning water. This wasn't a sandy beach sloping into playful waves. We were on top of a steep cliff, with giant stones all around. The water, filled with giant waves, was greenish blue near the cliffs, but turned to a dark blue as it got deeper. White spray and foam shot several feet into the air when the waves crashed into the rocks.

We had passed a little bay with waves gently licking a sandy shore a few miles back. Not so here. The waves were gigantic, and they angrily crashed against the cliff like they were mad that the earth was ending their journey east. The wind was so loud we had to almost shout at each other in order to be heard even though we were standing side by side.

Coming to the end was hard to take in emotionally and mentally. From the jail cell in Corinth, we had been heading here for just over a year. I felt a sense of accomplishment for getting here, and I felt a sadness for our quest that was now over. I was grinning, had a lump in my throat, and a tear ran down my face. We'd done it. But I was sure what *it* was, and I wasn't sure what to do now. Judea was another world—a different life. I wasn't sure who the me that stood at the end of the earth was. I was having a hard time believing that tomorrow we wouldn't get up and head west. We couldn't. We were there.

"It's hard to believe we can't go any further, isn't it?" I hollered at Acco.

He shook his head yes, and hollered back, "If we stay right here until sunset, we will be the last people in the world to see the sun today."

So, that's exactly what we did. We not only sat there until evening, we decided we would camp there for a couple of days. It felt right to tarry there, on what felt like sacred ground, and try to process the spiritual part of our journey. Perhaps we would be able to name how our long walk had changed us. I certainly needed to do a lot of processing.

A part of me was convinced a genuine healing had taken place in my soul. I had been devastated by Jesus's death, and I knew that I had regained my balance from that. I had accepted it as a reality and had come to terms with it. I knew I would now be able to honor him by attempting to live as he had taught us. That was real, but I wasn't sure how much I could attribute my change to the path. I still wondered if I had simply accepted a silly challenge to take a long walk so I could say I had seen something not many people from my part of the world had seen. But that was just a little lingering doubt. Most of me felt like I had somehow been called by something outside of myself to make this trip, and I was there for a reason, a reason that would bring great change.

That evening the ocean calmed, and, after we watched the sun sink into the ocean, we lingered by the edge of the cliff for a good while. Then we found a spot several yards up the slight hill at the top of the cliff, built a small fire, and cooked a couple of fish that we had bought from a young boy who had caught them in the bay we passed earlier that day. As it grew darker, we rehashed some of our adventures. Then we sat quietly for several minutes, looking into the fire. Finally, I asked Acco, "So, what's next?"

"What do you mean, 'What's next?'"

"I mean, I feel like a man without a purpose now. I'm not sure I ever felt like I had one before, but I never cared before. Now, I feel like I need to know what to do. I don't know what it is. So, what's next? We've walked to the end of the world on a sacred path, what do we do now?"

Acco nodded his head and took that in. I could tell he was having similar feelings, but then he chuckled and said, "I've got it! Let's do it the other way! Let's walk to the end of the earth in the east!"

He was laughing, and I knew he wasn't seriously proposing that we try to find the end of the world to the east, but I still said, "I'm out. One side of the world is enough for me. Besides, I think that journey is a good bit further. Mary once told me that some men from the east visited Jesus when he was a little boy, and they had been traveling for well over a year."

"Yes. They had traveled very far. They were stargazers and saw a sign in the heavens that a child that would change the world had been born," said a deep voice from outside our camp's fire light.

I almost jumped out of my skin. It took a couple of seconds for me to process that someone I couldn't see had joined our conversation. It took several more to take in that the person who owned the voice from the dark knew a detail about Jesus that not many did. After I gathered myself a bit, I tried to say in a calm voice, without much success, "Who's there? Step into the light, friend."

There was some baritone laughter, and then the owner of the voice stepped into the fire's ring and shouted, "I can't believe it's you! Why did you leave us? Where have you been?" It was James, the fisherman from Galilee, one of Jesus's closest friends. The last time I had seen him, we were watching Jesus be led away into the night.

I was dumbstruck. It was James. He was a bushier, wilder looking version of himself, but it was James. Of course, I guess I was a little bushier and wilder looking myself. I know Acco was.

"James! What? What do you mean what am I doing here? What are you doing here? Where's John? Are you alone?" The questions came out almost faster than I could ask them.

He kept laughing, pulled me to my feet, and gave me a big hug, "How good to see you! John's not with me. I guess he's still in Jerusalem with the others. I am by myself, and, to tell you the truth, I was getting a little lonely. So good to see you!" I didn't remember James being that much of a hugger, but I hugged him back and introduced him to Acco.

"I'm having trouble taking this in. I'm not dreaming, am I? What do you mean John is in Jerusalem with the others? Again, why are you here? The others? Why are the others still together? What are they doing in Jerusalem?"

James really laughed now. I had never heard him laugh like this. I wouldn't have thought my rough and tough friend had such a joyful laugh in him. "You left us when he was crucified didn't you? Friend, have I got some good news for you! He's alive! Jesus is alive!"

Oh no! I thought. James is the crazy man that the old couple in the village with the dogs told us about. Poor soul, surely he had been as devastated as I was. Apparently traveling so long by himself and being almost as far from home as he could possibly be had made him delusional. Of course it had. He said he was lonely. His mind was playing tricks on him. "Sit down James. Have some fish. Let me get you something to drink. Acco, do we have any wine left? Get James a little wine."

James laughed again, "I'll take your fish and wine, but I know what you're doing. You're trying to calm me down. You think I'm crazy. Everybody does, but hear me out. You were with us. You know what he was like. Hear me out. You won't think I'm crazy when I'm done. I know you won't. We saw him, talked to him. We touched him. I touched him! I heard you ask what is next, he gave us a mission and purpose. We saw him several times. Hear me out."

So, I heard him out. I gave him the whole night. Acco did too. James was so earnest that, even though I truly thought he had lost it, I wanted to hear what he had to say. Truth is, I was hoping so deeply that he wasn't crazy that I would have given him a week to convince me.

All night we listened. He told us that several people had seen Jesus alive. Several people had talked to him, and James gave us the details of every encounter.

Acco stuck to listening, but I had questions, lots of them. "What did he look like? What did he sound like? Are you sure it was him? How did he appear? Did he just walk up? Why did you sometimes not recognize him at first? How did he leave? Did he walk off, float away? Was his personality the same, had he changed? Were his wounds still there?" I peppered him with those and more.

James was patient, something else I didn't remember him being that good at, but he answered all my questions. He told us everything he could.

As the sun came up over the hills to our east, James stopped talking and looked at me. He looked at me deeply; it was almost one of those looks Jesus used to give. I could tell he was waiting for my verdict.

I poked the fire that was now mostly embers with a stick. I wanted to tell him that it was wonderful news, but, I had to be honest, "I don't know, James. This is a lot, a whole lot. I saw him hanging on that cross. I heard Simon say to make sure they were all dead by sundown. He was all but gone when I left, and you said yourself that he was dead, even put in a tomb. That he was there two nights. I don't know." I didn't say it but I was wishing that John or some of the others were there. I still hadn't ruled out that James was unbalanced.

"I believe him." It was Acco. It was the first time he had spoken for hours. He said it again, "I believe him." He was nodding his head up and down and had a look on his face that told me that he had made his decision. It didn't matter what I thought. Acco had decided.

"I don't think he's crazy, and I certainly don't think he's lying. I believe him.

"More than that, think about this. You have told me so much about Jesus I feel like I knew him too. He was wonderful, loving, and gave his life trying to let everyone know that they are loved by God. How could God let a man like that, a message like that, end in such a horrible way? How could that have been the last word in that man's life? I believe that he was somehow sent by God with a message, and it would be impossible for the last word to be that hate and fear are stronger than love. I believe James. And I now know what is next for me. I need to go home and tell my people, my family, that Jesus, the one you told us about, is alive. I need to tell them that not even death can kill love. Don't you see how good this news is? I believe him."

I looked at James, and there was a smile on his face and tears in his eyes. It was a look of gratitude. I imagined that I and the old couple in the village hadn't been the only ones to wonder if he was delusional.

I was lost for words. I wished I was like Acco. I wished I was like James. I wished I hadn't left Jerusalem when I did. I wished I could believe. But all I could muster was that I believed in Jesus's way of life and I loved him, but I couldn't believe that he was alive. I was sorry but I'd need something more than James's stories.

I figured that James and Acco were probably going to be talking about this for a while, and most likely trying to convince me to believe as they did, so I decided a long walk was called for. I told them I needed to be alone and headed south along the coast.

As I walked, I took in deep breaths of ocean air and listened to the waves crash into the cliffs to my right. I was hoping I could somehow find my balance and make sense of the last few hours. Oddly enough, I was open to the idea of ghosts and people encountering loved ones that had died. If James had told me that he had seen Jesus's ghost a couple of times, it wouldn't have been a problem for me at all. It's just that James was putting a lot more into his report of a risen Jesus than ghostly appearances from the other side. He was saying that Jesus was as alive, as alive as I was as I walked in the wind and sea mist, perhaps even more alive than that. He had died but now was alive and somehow giving James and the others strength to continue his work in their lives. James said that he was with us last night, that his spirit was with me the whole time I was walking. Try as I might, I just couldn't accept it. I wondered why. Wasn't the fact that Jesus was a good man and we would all do well to live like he did enough? Why did James have to add to it that he had seen Jesus, talked with him, and been blessed by him after the crucifixion? The crucifixion that I had seen.

It was mid-afternoon when I returned to camp. As I walked up, I had the sense that somehow a bond had been formed between James and Acco, and I wasn't a part. That felt very odd since I had traveled with Acco for months and even longer than that with James as we followed Jesus all over Israel. But, I was the odd man out.

"Hey, welcome back," said Acco. "Did you have a good walk?"

"It's beautiful here. Pretty hilly but wonderful. Yes, it was a good walk."

James smiled and said, "I remembered something I meant to tell you last night but never got to it. Judas is dead."

"Dead? How?"

"Killed himself, hung himself. We guess he felt so much guilt after helping them arrest Jesus, he couldn't bear it. We wish he had held on a few days. I really believe he and Jesus could have reconciled if Judas had been with us.

"Pretty sure we almost lost Peter too, but he and Jesus had a good talk and I think Peter was able to forgive himself."

"Forgive himself? For what?"

"You remember how Peter was promising Jesus that he could count on him no matter what that night when Jesus told us he was going to be arrested. Well, not even close. When they asked Peter if he was with Jesus, he denied it vehemently, more than once. I think if Jesus hadn't told him to remember what he said when he heard roosters crowing that morning, Peter may have ended it as well. He was devastated."

"It's very hard to not be who you really wish you were," said my occasionally very wise friend, Acco. I had to admit that, as details were added, James's story was starting to take on a feeling of truth, but still.

Over the next two days my feeling of being the odd man out in our group of three didn't go away. There was no reason for it to. James was totally focused on teaching Acco all he would need to know to walk in the way of Jesus. "Never show partiality. Always help people who are hurting if you can. Trust that prayer can bring healing. Don't just talk about faith, hope, and love, live them every way you can."

I thought to myself that Acco was already doing all that, but he was taking it all in like he was the world's thirstiest man and James had the best water around, so I let them talk and busied myself with preparing our meals and keeping the camp straight. I wasn't a part of their fellowship.

"James," I asked, "I still haven't quite figured out why you are here—how you got here."

He smiled and said, "Maybe the same thing got you and me here. Jesus told us to keep living like he had, to share God's love, reach out to people who are hurting, call people away from things that seduce us and take away our life. He said to go all over the world and do that, so I thought, why not as far west as you can go? I guess we were both somehow called to this place and the path that gets you here."

I nodded but then he added, "Or, maybe I am simply here for you. To tell you about Jesus being alive."

I shrugged, and, in an attempt to get the focus off me, I said, "So you are here, in this land, sharing, helping, and trying to tell people about Jesus? Moving around? Living like we did? How's that been?"

James paused and let out a little sigh, "It's been hard. Almost everyone thinks I'm crazy, and I get lonely sometimes. Very lonely. But, I'll tell you something that you may find strange since you aren't sure if I'm crazy or not yourself, I somehow find the strength to keep going because I feel like Jesus is with me, helping me. I believe he is."

"That's good, James. I'm happy for you." I reached over and put my hand on his shoulder, "I don't think you're crazy. I don't know what I think."

The next morning James announced he had had a dream that night that he believed was from God. Mary had appeared to him in a dream and told him that he needed to come back to Jerusalem, and he needed to leave as soon as he could. It didn't surprise me that Acco, my traveling companion, immediately said that he would accompany him east until the paths to Jerusalem and Acco's village parted.

Then they looked at me almost like they had forgotten me. I smiled at them, knowing our time together was at an end, and said, "James, I can't tell you how much it means to me that we somehow crossed paths here, go with God. Greet the others for me. Acco, you are the best friend I ever had. Tell everyone in the village, especially Mother, they will always be a part of me. You guys go ahead. I think I'll stay here awhile, still not sure what's next." I think they both were a little surprised that I wasn't going to accompany one or the other of them, but they didn't argue. There wasn't much to pack so early the next day we said our goodbyes, and I watched them walk east into the dawn's fog.

# One More Trip

LATER THAT DAY IT struck me pretty hard that I was alone, and I couldn't for the life of me come up with a good answer as to why I hadn't gone with Acco and James. At the very least I would have had companionship as I traveled back across Spain toward Gaul. Maybe, after a few weeks of walking with them, I would have decided to continue with one or the other when their paths separated. I had to admit it would have been good to see Acco's people again. I would have been very interested to hear what Mother made of James's story and Acco's belief in it. And, it sure would have helped me answer a lot of questions if I had gone with James back to Jerusalem. Looking back, I don't even have a good answer for why I didn't leave that afternoon and try to catch up with them. I am sure I could have. I just didn't.

When I did break camp, it dawned on me that I was officially a wanderer again. I wasn't following anyone, and I wasn't traveling with anyone, to anywhere. I had no destination. The only reason I started walking east was because the ocean was to the west.

I went east for a long time, then southeast for a bit, and finally south until I got to water again. For no particular reason I caught a ship for Rome, earning my passage as the ship's carpenter. Turns out, I didn't like Rome when I was there before, and I liked it even less this time. Too big, too loud, too many people impressed by their importance. I decided that the shorter the stay the better, so, after just two days, I went back to the port and hung out, trying to talk my way onto a ship to some place—any place. The first ship's captain that was willing to hire me was headed to Corinth. If there was a city in the world that I liked less than Rome, it was Corinth, but I took the job anyway. I guess that's just where I go when I'm lost. Maybe a part of me was hoping that I would do better on my third try.

The trip to Greece was unlike any trip on a ship I had ever taken. It didn't hold a single day of bad weather, and we always had enough wind to keep moving. It was such a peaceful journey that even Acco would have been hard pressed to find a reason to complain. The best and most beautiful day was the last day.

As we headed into the dock, the water was like crystal blue glass. It was so still you could see below the surface for several feet. It was easy to see the fish gathering around the ship's hull hoping something they could eat would drop. The sunlight was so bright and clean that, as I looked at the city from the ship's deck, I wondered if it had been given a good scrubbing while I was gone. Everything was so sparkling and pretty I decided that Corinth absolutely deserved another chance.

Once we tied up, I quickly grabbed my pack and disembarked. I began strolling aimlessly, trying very hard to give the city another chance. I am pretty sure this was the first time I was seeing it without the filter of too much wine.

As my feet and mind wandered, I wondered what Jesus would have thought of Corinth. Who would he have connected with? How would he act around pagan temples? It probably wouldn't take him long to make a new friend. It'd likely be someone that you would least expect.

As the sun got lower in the western sky, I realized that I was getting hungry, and I needed to find somewhere to spend the night. Since I had a little money, I tried to remember where a nice inn was. Just as one was coming to mind, I heard a child's voice, "Sir? Sir, help me please. Sir, please."

I looked in the direction of the voice, and there was a young girl. She couldn't have been more than seven, probably younger. It took me back a bit to realize that, even though the streets were fairly crowded, she was talking directly to me. Out of all the people in the street her appeal was for me only, "Sir, please help. My mother is sick and I am hungry. Please help." She acted like I was the only one there—her last hope.

I forgot all about seeking shelter and a meal. I was completely focused on trying to help this little girl. I confess that in the course of my travels I have walked past many beggars, even young ones, but there was no way I could pretend that I didn't see this child. I knew that she was not asking the world for help. She was asking me.

"What is it, little sister? How can I help?"

"My mother is sick," she said again. "She can't use her hands, and she is in so much pain. She can't die. Please help us. We are so hungry." With that the child broke into tears, started to sob, and sat down in the street. She seemed to have used all the energy that was in her to enlist my assistance.

"I'll do what I can," I pulled her to her feet. "We'll figure something out, little one. I'll help," I said as I gave her head a light hug. "I'm here. Take me to your mother. Let's see what's going on." That seemed to give her a little strength, and she led me into a small house that was nearby.

When I stepped inside, I couldn't help myself, I gagged. There was no other word for it but rotten. Rotting flesh. I knew immediately I was in the home of a seriously ill leper.

"Mama, I've brought someone to help us. We're going to be all right Mama. I've got a nice man who will help. See, Mama, here he is."

The poor woman was much weaker than her daughter. Her arms were covered with dirty bandages that had blood and fluid oozing through in places. I couldn't see her face because she had it covered, but I did hear the faint voice, "I'm sorry. We shouldn't have brought you here. But, my daughter," her voice tightened, "I couldn't let my daughter die. I'm sorry. Please don't leave."

"Mam, I am not going to leave, and your daughter is not going to die. What do you need? What can I do?"

"We have nothing. She's starving. Can you give her something to eat? Anything?"

I looked around and realized that when she said that they had nothing it wasn't much of an exaggeration. She must have slowly sold almost everything in the house, trying to survive in hopes that her disease would get better.

"We'll figure something out. I'll do what I can." I scratched my head, not at all sure what to do. "Let me get some water. I'll be right back."

I had noticed a relatively clean cistern nearby, and, after I found perhaps the last jug in the house, I went back into the street to get the woman and her daughter some water.

When I returned, I gave them both a drink and decided to take a look under the woman's bandages to see if there was anything to be done. I'm embarrassed to say that I probably grimaced when I touched them, but I did touch them, pulled them back, and found pretty much what I was expecting. She had lost a finger on one hand and most of her thumb on the other. There was no way to patch the skin on her arms. When I started to unwrap the cloth around her face, she turned her head and begged me not to, so I didn't. Judging from the rest of her, I didn't think it'd make much difference.

I rinsed the woman's bandages and tried to clean her a little, but it looked like infection had set in. I wrapped her back up as best as I could. Then I gave the little girl's face, arms, and legs a quick look and, miraculously, she looked clean, just starving.

"Okay, now that you are cleaned up a little, I am going to find some food. You both stay here, and I will be back as soon as I can."

The girl actually gave me a weak smile and nodded her head. The mother didn't respond at all. Changing her bandages had taken almost all of her strength.

When I got to the market, you would have thought I was buying food for a small army. I got bread, olives, fruit, and fish. One vendor had a little goat's milk and I bought him out. It was almost more than I could fit in my pack. In fact, I couldn't close it. Vegetables and wrapped meat were visible from its open top. I was determined that, if I could do nothing else, I was evicting hunger from that home.

When the house came into view, my heart sank. Standing right beside the door was the Roman soldier known as Marcus, the one who had cracked my head and thrown Acco and me into jail. He saw me too.

"Hey! I remember you! Street scum! What do you think you are doing? What are you doing with all that food?"

My mind raced as I tried to decide how to address him and what to tell him. Should I feign respect? Should I try to act casual? Should I think of a good lie or try to bribe him somehow? Nothing clever came to mind, so I just told him what was going on.

"A little girl and her sick mother needed some food, so I am trying to help them."

"Ha! Street scum, you are the worst liar I ever met!" He almost spit as he said it. He was disgusted by my very existence. To him, I was less than human. "I don't believe you for a minute! Where did you steal all that food?" He was moving toward me, confident and in charge. "You are under arrest, and this time you'll get more than a free night's lodging. Give me that stuff."

I struggled to find the words that would get me to the woman and her child, "Friend, I am not lying, and I am not going to give you this food. Like I said, it is for a very sick woman and her hungry child." I didn't mention that the woman was leprous. The last thing I wanted was for him to run them out of town. "I promise I didn't steal it. Let me deliver it, and I'll go back to the market with you, and the merchants will tell you that I bought it."

"You are stupider than I thought if you think I am going to let you go give that food to one of your street scum friends, probably that tall fellow you were with before, and then let you drag me back to market so you can pretend to look around and say the people you bought everything from must have gone for the day.

"Give me that pack right now. You're going back to jail. Your cell is waiting for you."

I am not sure what Jesus would have done, but here's what I did. It's probably not what Jesus would have done. I took my pack from my shoulder and extended my arm like I was handing it to him. When he reached for it, just before he could grab it, I dropped it and just as I hoped, he leaned forward, trying to catch it. When he leaned forward, I grabbed his head and threw him to the ground. As I did, I tried to jerk his helmet off but the strap was too secure and it stayed in place. Turns out, that was a good thing for him because, as he tried to scramble back to his feet, I was able to take his spear from him, and, as soon as I had both hands on it, I swung and hit him as hard as I could in the side of the head. I may have put a little extra on it, thinking Jesus and I owed him one. Anyway, the helmet helped, but not much. He went down in a heap. I was glad that he was right at their door because I was able to drag him inside and get him out of sight before anyone noticed.

The little girl stared at me blankly as I pulled and pushed Marcus into a corner. Her mother didn't move.

I offered no explanation for the unconscious Roman soldier. I just smiled and said, "Let me pour you some milk, little one. What would you like to eat?"

There were two cups left in the house but nothing like a plate, so I gave her some milk in one of the cups and a piece of meat between two pieces of bread that I broke apart. I figured that I could prepare a better meal after I looked at her mother. Nothing was coming to mind as to what to do about our unexpected guest.

Through all the soldier dragging and milk pouring, the mother hadn't moved or said a word. When I knelt beside her, I saw why. I guess she felt like having found help for her daughter released her from this world's duties. She was dead.

To say I was at a loss doesn't touch it. I was in a dead leper's house with an unconscious Roman soldier whose head I had tried to bash in, and a little girl was counting on me to keep her alive. "Lord God, help me," I sighed. I'll confess it was half curse, half sincere prayer.

"What in the world?" said what I assumed was an angel that appeared in the door.

"Aunt Priscilla!" cried the little girl as she jumped up and ran to hug what I now knew for sure was an angel.

Turns out the little one's name was Julia and her mother's, Helena. Aunt Priscilla, my angel, was Helena's sister and from out of town. She said that she had a dream a few days ago that disturbed her so badly she had to come and check on her sister and niece.

It was a lot to take in, but, after I quickly filled in the story for Priscilla, we decided she and Julia would take the food I had bought and go to the inn where I was headed before all this started. Early the next morning they would head back to the aunt's hometown. We really wanted Julia to be gone and impossible to find before she became entangled in whatever happens when someone knocks a soldier out and drags him into your house. Priscilla thanked me, gathered what little Julia had in the world, said a quick prayer over her sister's body, and took her little niece's hand and left.

After they walked out into the dusk, I looked down at Marcus and faced my dilemma. Say goodbye to Corinth forever right then, or try to help the man I had injured.

It wasn't an easy decision. A big part of my heart was already three miles out of town, but I knelt beside him, unbuckled the helmet, and gently slid it off his head. As I poured some water over the swelling spot on his head, I couldn't help but smile. It was almost exactly where he had bruised mine last year. I wondered if he'd just call us even.

I don't think you could call it regaining consciousness, but, with me helping, Marcus was able to stagger back to the jail. One of the soldiers saw us as we approached and asked Marcus what had happened.

"I don't know," he muttered.

"I don't either," I quickly said. "I just found him in the street near the market, and brought him here. I hope he's going to be okay."

"Help me get him inside," said the soldier.

We got him inside, and two others helped us get him into a bed in the soldiers' quarters. Soldier number one thanked me for bringing Marcus home. I said that I was glad to and took two steps toward the door and the safety of the night. Marcus said, "Wait! Stop him! Don't let him go. Arrest that street scum! I remember now."

# Right On Time

JUST AS MARCUS HAD predicted, I found myself in the same cell that Acco and I shared after our last encounter. This time I had it to myself, but this time I also had a chain collar around my neck that was connected to the chains around my ankles. For four days, I didn't see anyone except the jailer and him only briefly when he brought my meals twice a day. At first, I wondered why I hadn't met him the last time I was there. Then I remembered that they didn't feed us the last time I was there.

On the fifth morning, Marcus swung the door open in the manner that was apparently his habit, hoping to hit me or at least startle me. He smirked when he saw me jump, but not a word was spoken as he and another soldier chained my hands and made me shuffle to the magistrate's. He maintained his silence on our short trip, but he did seem to enjoy shoving me every chance he got. He grinned when I fell twice and struggled to get up. The other soldier wasn't Cornelius. He didn't grin, but he didn't care.

The magistrate told me that I was charged with resisting arrest and attacking a Roman soldier. Since I didn't have much of a defense, I decided to tell him the simple truth. I told him about the girl, her sick mother, and how I went to the market to get them some food. I told him I knew Marcus from when I was in jail before, and we hadn't hit it off. I apologized as sincerely as I could and told him that I wasn't thinking clearly, and didn't know what else I could do because I wanted so desperately to help Julia and her mother. The magistrate listened to my entire story without interruption, even nodding his head now and then. I wondered if he wasn't at least a little sympathetic to my predicament.

"Why would you risk so much to help people that you just met?" he asked. "You attacked a soldier, a very serious offense, to help a sick woman whose name you didn't even know."

"Yes sir. I wish I could have thought of something else to do, but I didn't. Why did I help them? I don't know what to tell you. I just wanted to help a little girl. A little girl that could have been my niece—a frightened little girl. I had a friend that said we're called to treat sick women and

106

hungry children like they're our own family. I guess I was trying to do that. I just know the little girl was desperate, and I wanted to do something."

"Sir, I have some things to add here, some things you need to know about this man." It was Marcus. The magistrate looked at Marcus in a way that gave me the impression that he wasn't a fan, but told him to go ahead. "Like he just said, I know him. I arrested him before and should have taken care of him when I had him, but kindness got the better of me. And, this friend he talks about? I knew him too. He was a man called Jesus the Galilean, and he was executed by Pontius Pilate in Jerusalem when I was assigned there. He called himself king and was trying to overthrow Caesar. I thought you might want to know that his friend didn't only teach others to help little girls and sick women. He was guilty of sedition."

"Sir," I said, "those were false charges that some religious leaders told Pilate because they wanted to get rid of Jesus. I was with him a long time and never heard him say anything that would make someone believe that he wanted anything that Caesar has. I assure you that the heart of his teaching was to love God, love others, and to do for others what you'd hope they'd do for you. Nothing more."

"This man's a liar! Everything he is saying is a lie! This Jesus was an insurgent, and so is this man. In fact, I don't believe there was a woman or little girl at all. I went back to that house yesterday, and it was completely empty. Who knows how long it has been that way?

"This man stole food, attacked me, is lying about everything, and is an obvious insurgent. He deserves nothing but execution, just like this teacher he thinks so much of, Jesus the Galilean." Then he turned to me, "I have asked you this before and you lied. Do you swear your allegiance to Caesar, or is your allegiance with your teacher, Jesus the Insurgent?"

Before I could say anything, the magistrate interrupted, "I'll ask the questions. You're obviously biased against this man. We seek truth and justice. We are fair here." But then he pretty much asked me the same question, "Are you loyal to Caesar and the empire, or should I believe that you are an insurgent like your teacher, this Jesus fellow?"

"Sir, again, Jesus was not an insurgent. His only crimes were that he told the truth, believed that every person is a person of sacred worth, and chose not to run from those that wanted to shut him up."

"Okay, Jesus is not on trial here, you are. What about you? How do you feel about Caesar and the empire? What do you say?"

I took a deep breath then, "Sir, I guess I'm with Jesus. Caesar and the empire don't have anything I want. I guess when it comes down to it, except for hitting Marcus, I am here because I was doing my best to live in the way that Jesus taught. I have told you my story. It is the truth. If you release me, I will be thankful, but I will leave here more determined than ever to live in the way of Jesus, and it seems likely I will be before you or another magistrate again one day. So, you can make of it what you will, but I guess I am saying that the way of Jesus is higher than the way of Caesar. I won't try to get into trouble, but that's where I am."

The magistrate clasped his hands and stared grimly at me for a few seconds. Then he said, "All right then, everything else aside, by your own admission, you attacked a Roman soldier. You may think the way of Jesus is higher, but the way of Caesar is stronger. From now on, when you walk in the way of Jesus, you will have thirty-nine stripes on your back. I sentence you to receive, at sunrise tomorrow, the forty minus one and to then be thrown on the street to see if anyone treats you the way you want to be treated."

"Sir," said Marcus quickly, "I am the one he attacked, may I be the one that administers his punishment?"

"Officer Marcus will administer the punishment," he said as he walked out.

Marcus and the other soldier escorted me back to my cell. This time there was no shoving, but Marcus did slowly count to thirty-nine.

Well, that wasn't something to look forward to. I had never seen the punishment given, but I had seen the back of a sailor who had been on the receiving end. This was going to be ugly. But, it could have been worse. I had come pretty close to confessing that I was an insurgent, and that would have meant death. I was young, pretty strong, and in good health. Perhaps, when Marcus was through and they let me go, I could somehow make my way back to the dock area and find someone that knew me. Most sailors that I knew would help me, if not for pity's sake, to thumb their noses at the empire. It wasn't going to be fun, but I'd survive.

That evening, it was Marcus, not the jailer, who brought my meal. I was surprised to see that it was a double portion. "I thought it would be good for you to have your strength up for tomorrow. It's going to be rough," he said. But, when I looked up at him, he couldn't fake his concern any longer. "Ha! It's going to be very rough, street scum. As rough as I can make it.

"In fact, I'm going to let you in on a little secret, just between you and me. You didn't really think I was gonna let you live after hitting me did you? I'm going to lose count tomorrow. Who knows when I will stop, but you know what? You won't be alive when I do. I know that much. Tonight is your last night. I wanted you to know," he said grimly then his shoulders shook with his silent laugh.

He sat down on the slab of a bed across from mine, "I think I'll watch you eat your last meal. I think I'll enjoy watching a man eat that knows I am going to kill him in just a few hours. You enjoy. I know I will."

I thought about making a break for it, but he had locked the door behind him, so, even if I somehow overpowered him, I would have nothing to do but sit and wait for the other soldiers to discover us. Then I could look forward to a legal execution instead of being murdered by Marcus.

I sat down as well and put the plate in my lap. That last meal we had with Jesus came to mind. Somehow it settled me a little that Jesus had not been afraid when he knew the end was coming. I decided to eat. I picked up a loaf of bread, broke it, and, for the first time in a long time, gave thanks as Jesus had always done.

"Want some?" I asked.

"No," he said with a smile. "I want you to eat it all. I want you to be strong, so you can last a long time tomorrow. I want you to feel every blow you can before you're gone."

"Why are you staying then?" I asked. "What do you want? Why won't you leave me alone? You've said what you had to say."

"No, I want more. I want to know what you are thinking, what you're feeling. I want to know that you're afraid. Are you afraid?"

"Yes. I'm afraid. Happy?"

"Are you angry?"

"Very much."

"I win?"

"You win."

He chuckled with delight. "What else? What are you thinking? Tell me, and maybe I'll kill you more quickly."

I thought for a minute. Why should I tell him anything? But then, I decided I'd tell him. "I'm thinking about Jesus. I was with him at his last meal. Somehow, he believed that death wouldn't win. I am trying to remember what he said, so I can believe that as well."

He laughed out loud. "That's the most pitiful thing I ever heard! Is it working for you?"

"Not totally, but a little." I think my honesty was starting to unnerve him.

"You stupid street scum. You are not only a liar and an insurgent, you're insane. Jesus is dead and tomorrow morning you will join him. What do you think he would think if he saw us right now? If he's your teacher, what would he want to say to me, the one that hit him, helped kill him, and is going to kill you?"

I thought about the last thing I heard Jesus say before I left. He was talking to Simon. "That's actually very easy. I know exactly what he would want me to say. Do you want me to say it?"

"I can't wait."

"Marcus, you are lost. You have no idea what you're doing, and I forgive you."

Pure hate looked at me, and I thought he was going to run me through with his spear right then. I kind of hoped he would. That seemed like an easier way to go, and I wasn't sure I would be able to hold my forgiving thoughts in the morning. But he didn't. Instead, he stood up, sneered at me and said, "See you in the morning, street scum."

I was by myself. I was afraid, and I was angry, but mostly I was sad. I did not want to die. I wanted to live some more. I wanted to see Acco again. I wanted to see my brother again. I wanted to know if James was crazy, or had he truly seen Jesus alive? I cried a little and gave up on my supper. I'm lying. I cried a lot. Then I did what they say you do when you know you are going to die. I reviewed my life.

I thought about days on the farm, my father, and how he had welcomed me when I came home. I thought about how I had broken his heart and ruined my relationship with my brother. My first meeting with Jesus ran through my mind, and then I thought about life with him. Those were wonderful days. Then a strange doubt came into my thoughts. Did all those things I remembered about Jesus really happen? I realized I had told those stories so much that I really didn't have a good memory of the actual events. My stronger memory was of telling the story. Had I embellished them? Had my grief made me tell things that weren't all the way true? Did I really see those things? Was he really as wonderful as I told Acco and the others he was?

I was about to spiral away when I decided I needed to claim something that I knew was true, something I could hold on to when the morning came. And there it was. I knew that whatever was factual in my memory, I loved. I loved Jesus no matter what was really real. I loved Acco and our time together. I loved James, Matthew, and all the others. I loved my brother, I loved Julia and her mother, I loved the life I had known since I met Jesus, and I loved enough that, yes, I forgave Marcus. He really was lost; there was nothing to be mad at. Love. It had to have come from somewhere. Whether that water had actually turned to wine or not, I loved more than I would have ever thought possible because I had known Jesus. I had something to hold on to. I was going to be alright. I guess love is stronger than death.

Then I felt him. It was just like when I felt him before I saw him at the wedding. He was there, with me. I knew he was there and I knew he could hear me. I realized I was smiling. "You're a little late don't you think?" I don't know if I actually said it or if I only thought it.

"Nope. Right on time." I couldn't see him, but he was smiling too.

My eyes were wet, but I was smiling, inside and out. "Well, thank you. Thank you so much." I remembered how Rachel had said thank you over and over that night at Simon's, and I got it now because that was all I knew to say—all I could say.

"Thank you," Jesus said back.

"Thank me? For what?"

I think he smiled again. "Thank you for helping Julia. Thank you for being a friend to Acco, for being honest with James, for standing true before the magistrate, for forgiving Marcus, and, most of all, for coming when I asked that day at the wedding."

The door swung open and I realized it was almost sunrise. This time I didn't jump, and Jesus didn't leave. I knew he wouldn't.

"You ready, street scum?"

"Yes. Yes, I am."

CPSIA information can be obtained
at www.ICGtesting.com
Printed in the USA
BVHW060212011122
650610BV00006B/20